Panchatantra

Author
Shubha Vilas

Wonder House

Table of Content

Mitra Bheda
(*The Separation of Friends*)

Mitra Labha
(The Gaining of Friends)

Kakolukiyam
(Of Crows and Owls)

Labdhapranasam
(Loss of Gains)

Apariksitakarakam
(Considered Actions)

Sometimes we are angry with ourselves and sometimes we are angry with others. Sometimes we create problems for ourselves and sometimes others create problems for us. How we respond to these situations of life, determines the quality of our personality. Anger, fear, greed, and pride are all negative aspects, and learning to deal with them with compassion can not only resolve problems but also make us better people.

From avoiding friendship with dishonest people to respecting everyone, Mitra-bheda teaches common sense through delightful stories.

Mitra Bheda
The Separation of Friends

1.1 The Curious Monkey

"Wow! What's that?" the curious monkey asked his friends.

Looking in the direction he was pointing at, all the monkeys saw what had attracted his attention. It was a log of wood!

"What's so interesting about a log of wood?" his friends asked.

Instead of answering them, the curious monkey ran to the log and jumped up on it. Looking at the wedge in the middle of the log, the monkey reached out to touch it.

A little farther away, a group of woodcutters were laughing and enjoying their meal, unaware of the prank the curious monkey was about to play. They had been cutting up this log of wood all morning and had managed to cut a part of it, but had to take a break for lunch. Not wanting the log to close up again, they had placed a wedge in the slit to keep it prised open.

This wedge was what the curious monkey began to tug at, while the other monkeys stepped aside. Suddenly the wedge snapped and the log of wood shut, trapping the curious monkey's leg!

While all his friends ran away in fear, the sad little monkey sat there in pain, waiting for the woodcutters to return from their break.

Lesson
Unnecessary interference in others' matters may interfere in the matters of your life.

1.2 The Brave Jackal

Gomaya, the jackal, was the hungriest he had ever been. It had been two days since he had eaten anything at all. His tummy was rumbling so badly! Just then he heard another rumble. A rumble that wasn't as faint as his tummy's. In fact, it wasn't faint at all. It was terribly loud!

In the silence of the forest, that thunderous rumble was a striking contrast.

Quickly, Gomaya hid behind a tree. Surely it must be some powerful animal lurking around in hunger, he thought. That rumble must be the rumble of his massive tummy. If caught, he wouldn't even fit into a corner of that animal's massive belly. Even king lion couldn't roar so loudly. This must be some new animal on the prowl. The more he thought, the more ghastly ideas came to his mind. Fear began to grip him from all sides.

Suddenly he had another thought. Why should he assume what the source of the sound was unless he could see where it came from? Gomaya took a deep breath, stepped out of his hiding place and stealthily moved towards the source of the sound. His heart was thumping loudly. All of a sudden he saw the source of the rumbling!

The next moment, Gomaya was rolling on the ground having a hearty laugh. It wasn't a fierce animal as he had expected. Instead it was a battle drum that had been abandoned in the forest, which was being beaten by a branch moving in the wind. As he walked up to the drum, he found a huge quantity of sumptuous food next to it that someone had left behind. Gomaya finally had a hearty meal!

Lesson

*When you walk towards the challenges
in life, success walks towards you.*

1.3 The Sweeper's Revenge

"I want revenge!" thought the royal servant as he lay in bed.

He had been insulted by a prosperous merchant of Vardhamana city. The merchant had thrown him out of his daughter's wedding reception simply because he had gone uninvited and sat in the royal arena meant for the king's family. Seething with anger, the royal servant spent all night planning how to avenge the insult.

Next day he went early to sweep the king's bedroom while the king was still in bed. Pretending to ignore the king, he muttered to himself, "What has the world come to... the merchant now dares to embrace the royal queen!"

The king went pale and asked him, "Did you see them together with your own eyes?"

The servant said dramatically, "O king, I have been gambling, and haven't slept all night. I am not in my senses. Please forgive me if I said anything wrong." He smiled to himself; his plan had worked well!

The king was greatly disturbed. The merchant was a highly trusted man in his office. He would have to take stern action if the sweeper's words were true. Why would the sweeper lie? He didn't even know the king was listening. He finally decided to take action and barred the merchant from entering his palace.

Next day, the guards stopped the merchant from entering the palace grounds. The merchant was surprised at the turn of events. He was clever enough to realize that the sweeper was somehow responsible for this trouble.

He invited the sweeper home, welcomed him with utmost respect and showered him with expensive gifts. He apologized profusely for his words and actions, explaining that the area he had entered during the wedding was a high security area and he could not have taken any risk in the king's security. Flattered with all the attention and gifts, he forgave the merchant and assured him that he would get him into the king's good books once again.

Next day while sweeping the king's bedroom, he enacted the same scene again, "How crazy the king is! Who eats cucumbers in the bathroom?"

The king was furious and he called the sweeper. "Have you seen me do that?" he thundered. The sweeper wept and said, "O king, please forgive me. I have been gambling all night, and

I'm sleep deprived. I may have said something inappropriate in my drowsiness."

The king then thought, "If he can speak nonsense about me, he may have spoken nonsense about the merchant too. Surely his words cannot be trusted. I have made a mistake in mistreating the merchant. I must call him back."

The king called the merchant, showered him with gifts and jewels and appointed him in his royal service again.

Lesson

Respect everyone, whether rich or poor, so everyone respects you.

1.4 The Sage and his Pouch

The sage and his potli were inseparable! They were like conjoined twins, joined to each other from birth. His potli – or pouch as you may call it – contained all the riches he possessed. He was a respectable sage as his name, Dev Sharma, suggested. People visited him at the temple where he lived, and brought gifts, food and money to offer him. He kept what he needed and sold off what was extra. All that money he kept in his string pouch, safely nestled under his arms at all times. He trusted nobody and the pouch never left his person even for a moment.

One day, a crook happened to eye the sage. Noticing that he never parted with his pouch, he got suspicious. What could that innocent looking pouch carry? Could it be a magic stone that gave unlimited wealth or did it contain a secret mantra for immortality? Whatever it was, it was worth having. By hook or by crook!

The next day he approached the sage and begged him to take him as his disciple. Deceived by the young crook's words, the sage agreed. The only condition was that he would not be allowed to enter the temple at night so he could meditate and chant in peace. The crook accepted the condition and the sage initiated him as his disciple.

Days turned into weeks and weeks turned into months as the crook did menial service for his guru. He massaged and washed his feet, cleaned the temple and arranged for his rituals. In spite of this, the sage still did not trust him enough to part with his precious pouch. The crook was frustrated and debated if it would be easier to just kill him and steal the pouch. Just then a villager came with an invitation for the sage to come for a thread ceremony to his house. The sage and the crook left immediately with the villager. On the way, the sage wanted to bathe in the river. He handed over his clothes and the pouch to his trusted disciple and waded into the river. The crook was overjoyed at the sudden turn of events. As soon as the sage was out of sight, he ran as fast as his legs could carry him.

When the sage returned, he was aghast to see his robes on the ground and his disciple nowhere in sight. It did not take him long to understand what had happened. There was no point in searching for him. Disappointed, he returned back home empty-handed.

Lesson
Do not judge a person simply by the sweetness of their words.

1.5 The Jackal who got Jacked

"**I** can almost predict what is going to happen!" a wise sage thought to himself, as he passed through a forest and witnessed a very intense scene. It all began with him hearing a loud thud. He turned to see if someone had fallen down and needed help. Just then he saw that it was the sound of two wild rams colliding head on.

The two rams were absorbed in a gruesome and bloody fight. As they ran around and continuously rammed into each other, blood oozed out of their heads and bodies. Unperturbed by their wounds, they continued to fight. In the vicinity, there was a hungry jackal. A few spurts of blood from the ghastly fight splashed on him.

The taste of blood glued him to the spot. The jackal began to helplessly walk towards the fight scene.

The sage, who was watching this from a distance, could clearly see that the jackal was doing the most foolish thing by walking towards the hostile rams. Even before the sage could react, the jackal was at arm's length from the warring rams. Licking its tongue, the jackal greedily looked at all the spilt blood.

Suddenly, the two rams moved closer and banged into each other once again. But this time, unfortunately, the hungry jackal was right in between them. The rams sped into him, hurting

him severely. His head, caught between such powerful forces, began to bleed severely.

The sage walked away shaking his head at the foolishness of the greedy jackal.

Lesson
Greed makes you oblivious to the obvious dangers lurking around.

1.6 The Crow's Enemy

The female crow was wailing. She had once again lost her children. This was the fifth time this had happened. Every time, the wicked cobra would come and devour her innocent eggs. She and her husband, the male crow, could do nothing to stop it. They were shattered. The only person they thought could help them during this calamity was their wise friend, the jackal.

As soon as they narrated their woes to the jackal, he made a profound statement. "There's no problem, however big it may seem, that cannot be overcome by wit."

Having said this, he gave them a plan of action. Soon the female crow was perched on top of a tree in the palace gardens. Timing her flight to perfection,

she swooped away a priceless diamond necklace which was lying on the ground next to a heap of clothes. The guards were busy guarding the queen's clothes while she was taking a bath. They were alert and kept a keen watch, making sure that no human ventured next to the queen's possessions. But little did they expect a crow to do that.

The queen saw something glittering in the air while she was immersed in the water. When she realised that the crow had flown away with her precious diamond necklace, she began to scream, alerting the guards. The guards immediately understood what had happened and began to chase the crow. The crow made sure that she flew at a pace at which the guards could easily follow her. She even stopped a few times, allowing the guards to catch their breath.

Finally, she brought them to the tree which housed her nest. Swooping down to the base of the tree, she dropped the diamond necklace into a hole that was hidden there. When the guards saw that the necklace was no more with the crow, they made their way to the hole and began to poke it to extract the necklace.

The black cobra residing inside that hole was fast asleep after a healthy meal of the eggs of the crows. Suddenly a shiny object slid into his hole and fell on him. A few moments later the snake heard a commotion outside. Human voices! Suddenly a stick slid into the hole and began poking here and there. The cobra had to act fast.

Immediately, he slithered out of the hole and coiled himself on the ground, and prepared his hood to attack. When the guards saw the cobra, they counter-attacked with sticks and stones. Surrounded from all

sides, the snake met his death without a chance to defend himself. The female crow shed silent tears of joy from above. It served him right. Just as he had eaten her helpless new-born babies, similarly he was beaten and killed helplessly.

Lesson

Real power lies not in physical strength but in mental strength.

1.7 The Clever Crab and the Cunning Crane

"**I** think I will die of hunger rather than of old age," the cunning crane muttered to itself. "What is the point of being so intelligent if I'm unable to feed myself?"

Old age had caught up to him fast. Much faster than the crane had expected. Gone were the days when he could stand in the lake and catch tons of fish in a day. He had great abilities then and a greater appetite. Though his abilities were gone now his appetite remained as fiery as ever! He had become extremely slow in his movements and his alertness had slackened considerably. Even new-born fishes were able to dodge him now.

Today his hunger had reached a height he had never experienced.

27

His tummy growled ferociously. Suddenly his growling belly gave him a brilliant idea. An idea that would surely fill his belly!

Walking up to the edge of the lake, the crane began to wail loudly. The sudden crying astonished the lake's residents. They swam away, distancing themselves from the melancholy crane. While everyone chose to stay away from the old crane, a wise and kind crab took pity on him. Crawling up to the elderly crane, the crab spoke gently.

"My dear uncle crane, why are you wailing like this? What misfortune has struck you? Please tell me what's troubling you so much."

On hearing the crab's gentle words, the teary eyed crane spoke between sobs, "My dear child, I have decided to renounce the world and fast unto death."

The crab smiled, sensing some melodrama from the crane. "Why would you cry if you have decided to do a noble thing like renouncing the world?"

"I do not cry for myself, O crabby! I cry thinking about the pain that all of you are going to feel soon." The crane's words piqued the crab's curiosity and he inched closer. So did the other creatures of the lake, to hear what the crane had to reveal.

Having made the desired impact on these creatures, the crane continued to share his woes. "All my life I have lived in this lake. This lake has been my home forever. But I can't bear to even think that this lake will soon be no more."

The crab was shocked. How could it be? How could a lake be no more? The crab inquired very seriously.

"Know that this news is absolutely true as I have heard it from the mouth of a wise astrologer visiting the vicinity of this lake. He predicted that there will be a twelve-year drought and this lake will dry up completely. Every living creature within this lake will die as a result." And the old crane began to wail even louder.

The crab was saddened on hearing the devastating news. Walking away from the disappointed crane, he went and discussed the grave situation with his friends in the lake. Everyone came to only one conclusion, to ask the crane to help them deal with this disaster.

"There is only one way to save yourself from this. I can take you to a much bigger lake a short distance away from here. That lake will not dry even if there is no rainfall for 24 years. Each of you could ride on my back and I can transport you to the safe haven," the crane spoke, showing great concern.

Not being able to think of any other solution, the fishes agreed to the crane's suggestion. Each day the crane took one of them to the promised lake. On flying a little distance away from the lake, he smashed them on a rock, devouring them to fill his belly. He would then return and tell tales about the happy life the fishes were living in the new lake.

After a few days, the crab expressed its desire to travel to their new home. The crane, bored of eating fish every day, was happy to have a change of diet. As they neared the stone used by the crane to smash his prey, the crab saw scattered heaps of bones around it. Immediately he understood the game plan of the wicked crane. Without panicking, he said to the crane, "Uncle, surely you must be tired by now. Why don't you take a break before resuming our journey?"

Having come this far, the crane was confident that the crab couldn't escape his clutches. As soon as the crane landed next to the stone and tried to hurl the crab onto the stone, the wise crab caught the neck of the crane with his powerful claws and strangled him to death.

Scampering back to the lake, the crab told his friends the entire story. Sad that they had lost many of their friends but happy that their lives had been saved by the clever crab, the fishes continued to live in the lake that never dried.

Lesson

When nothing else can help you in life, use your intelligence. Surely a solution will appear.

1.8 The Second Lion

The jungle animals were in a turmoil. Their lives had taken a miserable turn. Every moment, they lived in great fear. Finally deciding to end this constant fear, they decided to compromise with the lion king Bhasuraka. They proposed to send him one animal every day as his daily meal and in return he had to promise that he would stop hunting. He, of course, did warn them that if he didn't get his daily quota by the end of the day, he would surely kill all the animals as he wished. Though every day one of them died, the rest lived peacefully till their turn came.

Next, it was the turn of a little hare to offer itself to the lion. Having just begun life recently, the hare was not at all prepared to die. Unfortunately, he had no choice but to go. He walked slowly

towards his death. Not willing to die so fast, he crawled like a tortoise to delay his fate, thinking all the while. The lion's patience was waning and he was furious at the non-arrival of his daily food quota. As he was pacing back and forth, the little hare reached, walking very slowly.

The lion leapt to pounce on it, but the hare stopped him mid-air by saying something shocking. "If it was not for the other lion, you would have gotten to eat five hares today."

That shocked the lion. What did he mean by "other lion"? Wasn't he the king of the jungle? How could there be another lion in the same jungle? Walking up to the hare, the lion bent low so his face was almost touching the face of the hare. The hare wasn't even worth a single bite. The animals definitely wouldn't be foolish enough to send just one hare as the daily quota.

He wanted to know details of what this tiny hare was talking about. In a soft voice, the hare explained that as the five of them were on their way to offer themselves to him, they were stopped by another lion who claimed to be the real king of the jungle and called him an imposter. The king lion was furious about the existence of a competitor who had dared to insult him.

The hare further revealed that that second lion captured four of the five hares and dared the first lion to come and claim them after defeating him. The hare finished his explanation by saying that the second lion had left him only to pass on the message of his challenge to the first lion. By then the king lion was fuming in anger. His dominion had been challenged. He declared that he would eat only after finishing off his enemy.

As they made their way towards the other lion's abode, the hare warned him that the second lion lived in an impenetrable den. A hideout that was very difficult to break into. Moreover, the hare cautioned him that the other lion seemed a lot more powerful too. Uncaring for all the warnings, the king lion urged him to hurry up and take him there.

The hare led the lion to a deep well. Pointing to the well, he declared that this was indeed the home of the second lion. In great anger, the lion stepped up and looked into the well only to see his own reflection in the water. Seeing the face of a lion stare back, he began to roar loudly. The echo of the well made it seem like the lion below was roaring even louder.

The lion decided to end the dispute by leaping inside the well and killing his enemy. Little did

he realise that it was his own reflection. The well was too deep for the lion to swim or even come out of.

That was the end of the tyranny of the lion and the beginning of peace in the jungle. The little hare become a hero overnight.

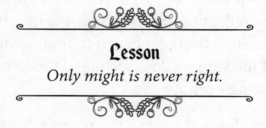

Lesson
Only might is never right.

1.9 A Flea, a Bug, and a Promise

"**I** promise," pledged the bug solemnly to the flea. The question was, would the bug live up to her promise?

The bug had intruded on the peaceful life of Mandavisapini, a white flea living in the silken folds of a bedsheet on a king's bed, feasting on royal blood.

Mandavisarpini had warned the bug of the lurking dangers if caught, but the bug was determined to stay. She had counteracted the warning saying, "Madam, a guest is welcomed with sweet words and refreshments, not like this. I crave to taste the blood of a king. How sweet it must be… nourished by the best of foods! Please let me fulfil my desire."

Mandavisarpini was unrelenting, "Your bite is like a sharp needle and will awaken the king from sleep. Do you promise to bite only after he is in deep sleep?"

And the bug had given her word. The flea found no reason to doubt her. Trusting her, together they waited for the king to come. As soon as the king lay supine, the bug quickly forgot all about her promise and rushed to satisfy her craving for blood. No sooner had she bitten the king than he sprang up wincing in pain.

He clapped for his servants, who came rushing in. The cunning bug hid herself while the naive flea was caught between the folds and killed immediately.

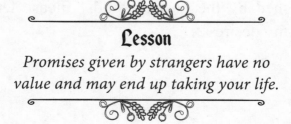

Lesson

*Promises given by strangers have no
value and may end up taking your life.*

1.10 The Blue Jackal

"There is a new animal in the jungle. Have you seen it?" Every animal small or big was only discussing this. They were all terrified and confused. Not knowing how to react to this unknown calamity, they decided to come together and deal with the issue at hand. Without knowing the strengths of this new animal, no one wanted to risk confronting it.

While they were busy discussing this serious issue, unknown to them, they were being watched by the new animal who was unable to control his laughter. It was no new animal but an ordinary jackal. While running to save his life from a group of street dogs that were chasing him, he had run into the home of a washer man and, by mistake, had jumped into a vat of blue dye. As a result, he was fully blue in colour now. All the animals had mistaken him for an alien animal and were afraid of him!

Yes! For a change everyone feared him. The blue jackal was mighty pleased with how the tables had turned. He wanted to take full advantage of this situation. Making a dramatic entry into the meeting arena, the blue jackal walked with his head held high. Turning to face his audience, the blue jackal spoke.

"Lord Brahma has personally created me. There is none like me. Being a special creation of the universal creator, he has asked me to take charge of all the animals. He sent me here to rule the world. I invite all of you to reside in my kingdom in peace and harmony."

On hearing the lofty speech of the blue jackal, the animals unanimously surrendered to him. The thrilled jackal immediately assigned roles to each of the animals. He made sure that everyone did something for his pleasure. He also made sure that all the jackals were driven away from the jungle. He didn't want any of them to come anywhere near him for the fear of being recognized.

Many months passed in joy for the blue jackal and the animals had accepted him as their king wholeheartedly. One night everything changed all of a sudden. The other jackals began to howl from a great distance. In the silence of the night, the sound of the howls reached the ears of the blue jackal who missed his jackal days and habits terribly. Unable to control himself, he too joined the howling. He cocked his head up and howled loudly in unison with the other jackals!

When all the animals saw their king howling like an ordinary jackal, they realized that they had been cheated by him all along. Joining forces, they caught him and beat him black and blue.

Lesson

When you cheat your own people, you
will be beaten by your own people.

1.11 The Guest Camel

"**W**ho is that strange looking animal in my jungle? Is it an alien wanting to take over my kingdom or is it a robot sent by mankind?" wondered the lion aloud. Madotkata, the lion, was the king of this tropical jungle and was on his usual morning walk with his coterie of followers, the crow, the jackal and the leopard, amongst a few others.

"No, your sire," said the well-travelled crow. "It is a camel. I have seen it in villages and it may have lost its way. I've heard its flesh is delicious. Let us kill him and feast on him."

"No, no!" exclaimed the lion. "He is a guest in our jungle. How

can we kill our guest? Please go and bring him here. We will not harm him."

The camel was brought and he bowed in front of the lion. He had been separated from his caravan while crossing the jungle and wished to go back home. But the lion suggested he stay in the jungle as a guest and feed freely on the lush grass; why go back to slavery? The camel agreed and became a part of the lion's close group of animals.

One day, the lion was severely injured while fighting a mad elephant. So much so that he was immobile, unable to hunt for survival. His followers were alarmed, because without the lion in action, all of them would perish without food. They searched for weak and sick animals for the injured lion to prey on, but in vain. The hungry jackal then suggested slyly, why waste time in searching for animals when they could prey on the camel amongst them. The lion refused to do so. "It is against my principles to attack a guest. It will be a sin." He emphasised firmly.

But the jackal was not one to give up. "What if he himself surrendered to you? It would not be a sin to kill him then," he argued. The lion could not refute the logic, and said, "Do what you think is best for everyone."

The jackal had a master plan ready. As per plan, the crow spoke first. "Your highness, we have not found any animals for you. But I offer myself to you to save you from hunger. Please eat me immediately."

The jackal interrupted him and said, "You are so small that your flesh will not be enough for him. So I offer myself. Master please accept my offer to surrender and save yourself from hunger. By sacrificing myself, I will surely go to heaven."

The lion shook his head sadly, refusing the offer. One by one, the other animals offered themselves. The lion refused all of them. The camel was observing all of this. He was inspired to offer himself too as the lion was refusing everyone anyway. He spoke loudly, "O king of jungles, how can you eat other carnivore friends of yours? But you can eat me. I offer myself to you and take this opportunity to go to heaven."

All the animals cheered in appreciation. The lion jumped on the camel and quickly killed him. The animals happily ate to their heart's content.

Lesson

It is dangerous to be in the company of wicked people. Even their sweet words can be poisonous.

1.12 The Sea and the Eggs

There was tension brewing in the nest of the tittibha birds. Mama bird was extremely angry with papa bird. It was March, the time to lay her eggs. All she wanted was a safe place for her eggs to hatch. Was she asking for too much? But papa bird, who was too lazy to relocate, said, "My dear, we live on the beautiful seashore, the best place for you to lay eggs. Our children will love the sound of the waves."

"But the high tide will snatch away my eggs even before they hatch. It is powerful enough to drown an elephant! Don't you understand?" argued the mama bird. Alas, he was just too stubborn. He assured her, "I shall see how the sea dares to take away our eggs. I give you my word, our eggs will be safe." She sighed and gave in to his decision of staying at the seashore.

The sea heard the conversation between mama and papa bird and wondered how a small bird like the tittibha could protect his eggs from her. She decided to take his eggs away to see what he would do. That would be fun!

Soon the eggs were laid and mama bird did everything she could to care for them. One day when she was out to bring food, the sea made waves that became bigger and bigger and lashed at the shore and swallowed the eggs. When mama bird returned, the nest was empty. She wept and wept and blamed papa bird for the mishap. "Why didn't you listen to me when I told you the seashore was a dangerous place?"

But papa bird was confident about retrieving the eggs. He said, "Don't worry, mama bird. I will bring our eggs back from the sea."

How would he do that? "By drying up the sea! I will drink all the water of the sea, day and night, and empty the sea."

Mama bird didn't know whether to laugh or cry. She called all their friends, the crane, the peacock, the swan and others. They all agreed that it was impossible to dry up the sea. And the best thing to do was to approach the king of birds, the mighty Garuda, the vehicle of none other than Lord Vishnu. "He can tell us what to do. He may even come and help us dry the sea." They all chirped in unison.

The birds set out to meet Garuda. They explained their predicament to him, "You are our protector. Please save us from the sea."

The Garuda was very alarmed. The sea had indeed tried to wipe out the avian race by swallowing the eggs. He sent a message to Lord Vishnu that his race was in grave danger and he could not report to work till he had solved the problem. Lord Vishnu, being concerned, came to talk to Garuda himself. And then all of them went to talk to the sea.

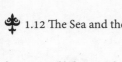

Holding the thunderbolt in his hand, Lord Vishnu rebuked the sea. "You have done a wicked act by swallowing tittibha's eggs! I order you to release her eggs at once or face my anger."

The sea was terrified to see Lord Vishnu himself. Apologising profusely, she begged for forgiveness and humbly returned the eggs.

Lesson
A strong mind can achieve the impossible.

1.13 The Flying Turtle

"**A**re you sure this is going to work?" one of the friendly swans asked Kambugriva, the turtle. The turtle smiled and nodded his head enthusiastically. The second friendly swan said, "I'm not so sure, with a talkative turtle like you."

Kambugriva shook his head in disagreement. "I am wise enough to know when to open my mouth and when not to." Besides this was his own idea, so naturally he would comply.

The three friends had been discussing a solution to a great problem they were in. The lake in which they had grown up, right from the day they were born, was drying up. There hadn't been bountiful rainfall in years. If this trend continued, in a few months, there wouldn't be a single drop of water left in the lake.

The turtle had suggested that the swans fly around and look for an alternate source of water. This suggestion had led them to the discovery of a huge lake with plenty of water at a distance from where they were. The swans could easily fly back but the question was how the turtle would ever reach there. That's when the turtle had an idea. He asked them to find a tough stick. His idea was to have both the swans hold the ends of the stick in their mouths, and he would hang onto the middle of the stick with his. Thus the three friends would fly their way to freedom and happiness.

Unsure of the plan but sensing the confidence of the turtle, the swans agreed. As per their plan, the swans carried the turtle hanging onto the stick. When they reached mid-air, the turtle experienced a joy unlike any other in his entire life. There was so much he wanted to tell his friends about his feelings right then, but he realized that he had to keep his mouth shut.

As they flew over a village, some villagers happened to see this unique sight of two swans carrying a turtle on a stick. They began to gather in hundreds and loudly expressed their surprise

and wonderment at the unique friendship between the animals.

The turtle became curious on hearing all the commotion below. Especially when he saw that everyone was pointing in his direction and talking animatedly. He was dying to know what they were saying. The wind was blowing so hard in his ears that he could hardly hear anything. He decided to check if his friends could hear anything at all.

"What is all this …?" Kambugriva fell straight to the ground as soon as he opened his mouth. The swans helplessly watched their friend fall right in the midst of the villagers, who rushed in hordes to capture the turtle.

Lesson
Overconfidence in yourself and neglect of advice causes a downfall.

1.14 The Four Small Friends Topple a Big Enemy

In one moment, their happiest day had become their saddest day. The sparrow couple had been in the midst of celebrating their greatest joy. The birth of their first set of children. This had indeed been a momentous occasion and they were dancing around from one tree to another celebrating their happiness. Suddenly they heard an uproar. The ground began to quiver. Initially they couldn't understand what was happening. The worried parents rushed to their nest to protect their newly laid eggs.

Just as they reached there, they spotted the cause of the chaos. It was a mad elephant. The heat had upset it and it wasn't coping well. Out of sheer frustration, the elephant was on a rampage, destroying everything in its vicinity, trees included. Right in front of the aghast parents, the elephant broke down several trees and was rushing towards the tree on which their nest was situated. The bewildered parents desperately tried to hold on to their eggs while the elephant was bulldozing the tree. The sparrows were tiny and the tree was massive. As the tree began to collapse, they had no option but to let go and fly off to save their own lives.

The sparrows were heartbroken. The female sparrow wailed so loudly that the entire forest came to a stand-still. Even the crazy elephant stood still for a moment looking in her direction. Only till the heat caught on and his madness took over once again. Hearing the pitiful cries of the female sparrow, a woodpecker who was in the vicinity was stirred.

Flying up to her, the woodpecker said, "My dear sister sparrow, crying will not do you any good. Your children won't return if you cry. The will of destiny can never be changed."

The sparrow spoke between her sobs, "I understand that very well. I am crying more because while that cruel elephant was wreaking havoc in my life, I could do nothing but watch helplessly. I may not be able to bring back my children, but I do want to avenge their death. Please help me."

The woodpecker immediately directed her to a fly who was a friend. The fly introduced them to a frog who was a friend. Soon, a team of four friends gathered to achieve a common goal. The wise frog explained to the others that although all four of them were individually small and helpless, together they could destroy the most powerful forces. All of them simply had to play their parts in a grand plan.

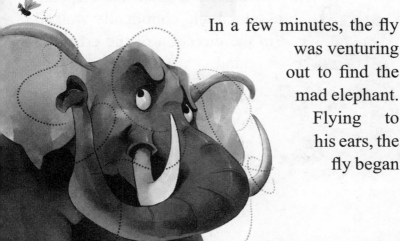

In a few minutes, the fly was venturing out to find the mad elephant. Flying to his ears, the fly began to harass him with its buzzing. The elephant was initially not bothered about a tiny fly hovering around his ears. But when it got persistent and very close to his ears, the elephant got irritated. He tried to shoo it away by waving his ear lobes and his trunk. But the fly was too persistent. In order to gather his patience, the elephant closed his eyes. As soon as his eyes shut, the woodpecker swooped to the head of the elephant and pierced the elephant's eyes with its sharp beak.

The pain maddened the elephant. He began to run around helplessly, unable to see anything before him. The heat and the pain together caused unbearable thirst so he looked for a source of water to quench his parched throat. Suddenly he heard the croaking of a frog. Surely there must be a water body around, the elephant assumed and confidently walked in the direction of the croaking sound.

When the elephant edged near, the frog stepped away and the elephant walked into a deep dark well that

had no water. The
elephant suffered a
lot inside the well with
no help whatsoever.

The four friends smiled,
having accomplished
their task. Though the
sparrow's children
would never come
back, she felt justice
had been served
by punishing the culprit. She lost her eggs but
gained many friends.

Lesson

*The biggest of tasks become the simplest
of tasks if we work together.*

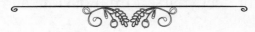

1.15 The Angry Monkeys

The bird had never seen anything so funny in her entire life. From her nest she could see a group of monkeys trying to light a fire. It was pouring cats and dogs and the monkeys were shivering from cold. What was funny was that they were trying to light a fire with the gunja fruit. Just because the fruit was red it did not mean it could ignite a fire. What fools! She laughed heartily at their stupidity.

Controlling her laughter, she hopped down from her nest to inform the monkeys that their efforts were futile. "These are gunja fruits, not embers of fire," she squeaked as loudly as she could. "Don't waste your time on this. Go and find shelter in a cave to protect yourself from the rain and cold."

The monkeys were irritated with the bird. They were already wet, hungry and frustrated. They had no desire to take advice from a nobody. "Go away!" they tried to shoo her away.

The bird ignored them and hopped closer to the ground, and gave her motherly advice again. "Stop it, stop it. There's no point in doing this," she persisted. The monkeys scowled at her and told her to get lost. Determined to  stop them, the bird hopped closer. She chided them again but by then the monkeys had lost their temper. One of the monkeys caught her by the neck and flung her to the ground. The poor bird was gravely injured for trying to help the monkeys.

Lesson

It is foolish to give advice when no one wants it.

1.16 The Bad Friend

Papabuddhi was pacing in his house. His mind was churning. For the last hour or so he had been deep in thought. The only time he actually thought was when he was hatching an evil scheme. The rest of the time he hated taxing his brains. He always felt that when life could be lived lazily then why must one work hard. His way of life was to make others work for him while he lazed around. His family was in dire need and he had to hatch a plan soon. If he didn't manage to make some quick money then he would have to take up the path he hated, the path of hard work.

That's when his friend, the innocent, intelligent and hardworking Dharmabuddhi passed by his house. As soon as his eyes fell on his pious friend, an idea struck him.

He ran up to Dharmabuddhi

and caught his arm. A surprised Dharmabuddhi stopped in his tracks to listen to his friend. Papabuddhi spoke his mind, "My dear friend, why don't we earn some good money by travelling to far off kingdoms which will take care of us during old age? No matter how much we stay in this village, we will always be in need. Besides, we will never gain experience and worldly knowledge to share with our grandchildren if we stay like ducks in this godforsaken village. Let us venture out and make a fortune, and return to spend the rest of our lives in fun and frolic."

The two friends agreed to venture out to a kingdom they felt had the highest potential to give them their desired fortune. Seeking blessings of the elders, they left on their voyage. As per their plan, Dharmabuddhi's skill, knowledge and hard work earned them much more than they had expected to earn. Soon they were on their return journey with a plethora of experiences and a huge stash of wealth.

Just as they reached the precinct of their village, Papabuddhi suggested that they hide their wealth in a mutually agreeable place and not carry it all into the village. He feared theft and more than that the unreasonable requests that all their friends and relatives would make. Dharmabuddhi agreed to his friend's proposal and they buried most of their wealth in the forest under a chosen tree. Agreeing to return together when they required it, the two friends entered the village with minimal money.

A few days later, the crafty Papabuddhi made his way to the hideout and dug out all the money. Bringing it back with him, he hid it in a safe place within his house. The next day, he went to his friend feigning that he needed money urgently. When they both reached their hideout, they found the wealth missing. Papabuddhi began to vehemently accuse Dharmabuddhi of stealing all the wealth. Dharmabuddhi was aghast at the accusation and utterly denied any role in the absence of the wealth.

Papabuddhi ran to the village heads and lodged a complaint against his friend. The village elders told both the men to take a pledge on the fire-god proclaiming that they were speaking the truth. Papabuddhi suggested that instead they could request the spirit of the tree below which they hid the wealth to be the witness of the theft. He felt that surely the tree would reveal the identity of the culprit. The village elders found logic in his suggestion and decided to give it a try. If that failed, then they would make the two friends take a pledge before the fire-god.

Papabuddhi had thought this out well. He had already asked his father to hide in the hollow of the tree and speak as if he were the spirit of the tree. Accordingly, when asked who the real culprit was, the father spoke in a mystical voice and put the entire blame on Dharmabuddhi. Everyone was dumbstruck hearing the tree actually speak.

They decided that now there was no way to deny the fact that Dharmabuddhi had actually stolen all the wealth that rightfully belonged to both of them.

As they were discussing how to punish Dharmabuddhi appropriately for his mischief, Dharmabuddhi began to wonder. How could the tree speak? And even if it were the spirit of the tree speaking, why would it lie? He went around the tree for a closer look. That's when he noticed the hollow at the back of the tree. He gathered a heap of dry grass and placed it at the mouth of the hollow. Setting it on fire, he stood aside to watch the outcome.

As the fire began to flare up, Papabuddhi's father couldn't bear it anymore. The smoke and the heat were killing him. He ran out of the hollow partially burnt, and began to roll on the ground to stop the fire from completely burning him. Everyone was dismayed at the turn of events. When they caught him and inquired, the shaken father revealed his son's plan. Thus Papabuddhi's mischief was caught and he was punished appropriately. The village elders congratulated Dharmabuddhi for his quick-wit that not only saved his life but also brought justice to the wrong-doer.

Lesson
Friendship with dishonest people
comes at a price.

1.17 The Foolish Crane that Invited Trouble

The mother crane was so overcome with sorrow that she wanted to die. How could she go on living while her children were constantly dying? She begged and pleaded with the father crane to do something about the black monstrous snake that lived under their lavish home in the huge banyan tree. The black snake would climb up the tree and devour her innocent children one by one and she could not bear the grief.

A crab nearby heard the mother crane weeping. "Why do you cry like this, O mother crane?" he enquired. The crane narrated her woes to the sympathetic listener. The crab was clever and thought that he could get rid of both, the snake and the crane, in one stroke. Both were his natural enemies and life would be peaceful without them.

He said to the crane, "Hear me now. I will tell you how you can help yourself. Scatter some dead fish and animal flesh outside the snake's burrow. When the mongoose smells the food, he will come looking for it. When he finds the burrow, he will not hesitate to fight the snake and kill it."

The crab did not reveal to the crane his sinister intentions behind this plan. The grief-stricken crab took his suggestion and did as instructed. As per the plan, the mongoose followed the food trail and killed the snake in the fight that ensued. The mongoose then saw the numerous cranes residing on the tree. He went after the cranes one by one, and in due course, he killed the cranes too. That was the end of the cranes as well as the snake.

Lesson
The solution to a problem should not worsen the problem itself.

1.18 The Rat that Ate Iron

The merchant's eyes gleamed. He was overcome with pure greed when he saw the antique iron balance in front of him. The piece was invaluable and here it was being offered to him by his friend's son, Jveernadhana.

"Uncle, I need money to travel far and wide in search of a better living. Here's my ancestral iron balance, I want to mortgage it in return for my travel expenses." Jveernadhana's words fell like music on his ears.

He gave him the money, controlling his urge to dance and jump and shout with joy. He took possession of the antique with a singing heart. He would not part with it even if Jveernadhana came back and returned the loan. Months turned into years and one day, much to his dismay, Jveernadhana was back at his doorstep.

"Uncle, here's the money I borrowed from you. Please give me back

my iron balance." Without looking at him, the merchant replied, "There were too many rats last year and they ate up your balance. I'm sorry, I had to throw it away."

Jveernadhana was no fool. He knew the merchant had swindled him. He kept his emotions under control and said, "It's okay, uncle. I'm going to the river for a bath. Can you send your son along to keep an eye on my clothes while I take a bath?"

"Sure," said the merchant, relieved at how easily he had convinced Jveernadhana with his lie. He called his son, happy to send him for the simple errand. But Jveernadhana had a plan. After taking a bath he led the boy to a cave and locked him inside by placing a boulder at the entrance. He went back to the merchant and said, "While I was taking a bath, a flamingo swooped down and carried your son away. I'm sorry but your son is gone."

A flamingo carried a boy away? The merchant was seething with anger. "You liar! That's next to impossible. Tell me what happened or I shall complain to the village elders." He dragged Jveernadhana to the village courtyard and approached the elders, narrating the impossible incident told by Jveernadhana.

"I demand justice from the village elders. This rogue has kidnapped my son! How can a flamingo carry a grown boy?" he wept in front of them. The council looked at Jveernadhana questioningly. Jveernadhana was quick to reply, "In a village where rats can eat iron, why can't a flamingo carry away a child?"

Now everyone looked at the merchant for an explanation. Jveernadhana explained how the merchant had stolen his iron balance citing that

rats had eaten the iron. To get his belonging back, he had concocted the story of the flamingo carrying away his son.

The merchant turned scarlet red with embarrassment while all the villagers applauded Jveernadhana's intelligence. They ordered the merchant to return the iron balance and peace was restored.

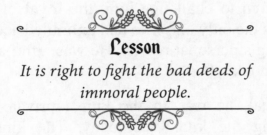

Lesson
It is right to fight the bad deeds of immoral people.

1.19 The King and the Foolish Monkey

"Take that, you evil fly," cried the excited monkey as he brandished his sword in the air. Slashing the sword all around him, he enthusiastically followed the fly to annihilate it. He was determined to win the battle against this fly that had dared to challenge him, the royal monkey. He was the only one who had unlimited access to the king's personal rooms. He was, after all, the royal monkey!

As usual, he was in the king's private room enjoying the king's company. The king had fallen asleep. That's when this insignificant fly had entered the out-of-bounds room and sat on the king's chest. The monkey tried to shoo it away but the fly kept returning, as if mocking his authority. That had really angered the monkey. Whoosh! He attacked the fly with a sword. He hit with all his might this time. The fly escaped unhurt while the king was rudely awakened with a long gash across his chest, courtesy of his foolish pet monkey.

Lesson

The helping hand of a foolish friend is worse than the kick of an enemy.

1.20 The Thief and the Brahmins

"**O**m purnam idam purnam adah; the supreme lord is complete by himself and so is this world created by him…" such sweet words poured out from the mouth of the thieving Brahmin.

Quoting from the Sri Isopanishad, a holy scripture, he was able to impress the four Brahmins who had come from another town. By reciting scriptures fluently with an innocent face, he was an expert at getting his way. He slyly asked them to employ him as their assistant to which they readily agreed.

Once they had finished their business, they debated on how they should carry the money they had earned. Not wanting to risk anything, they decided to buy jewels with all the money and hide it in a secret place. The thief Brahmin was shocked to see them cut open their thighs to hide the jewels and seal the skin with a special ointment they carried. There was no way he could steal their riches now. He had to think of a plan soon or he would be left twiddling his thumbs.

The next morning, at the time of their departure, he started to weep. "My friends, how will I live without you? My heart has grown fond of you and refuses to live alone. Please take me with you." He cried, shedding crocodile tears, thinking of how he would get ample opportunities to steal their jewels on the way.

The four Brahmins were touched by his emotional display and took him along. They soon reached a jungle where they found themselves surrounded by a bandit tribe who had a magical crow who could smell treasure. The crow screeched, "They are carrying treasure. Kill them, kill them!"

The bandits captured the five Brahmins and searched them thoroughly. Alas, no treasure was found. Even after removing their clothes, they found nothing. "The crow has never been wrong. Hand over your treasure or I will cut open your stomachs and find it!" threatened the bandit chief.

Startled by the sudden turn of events, the thief thought fast. "They will surely kill me too. They won't find any treasure inside my body but I will be dead by then. Should I try to save the others?"

Aloud, he said, "It would be wrong to kill all of us based on your crow's words. I offer myself to be killed so that you know we have

no treasure with us." The bandits killed him and searched his body but they found nothing. The chief apologised to the other Brahmins and spared their life. "I'm sorry I killed your friend. My crow has never made a mistake till today. Please continue your journey."

The four Brahmins felt grateful to the Brahmin who had sacrificed his life to save them.

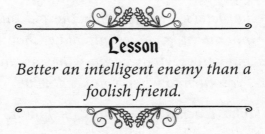

Lesson
Better an intelligent enemy than a foolish friend.

In the modern era, we get attracted to people who are rich and famous. But our heroes might not have strong characters. This is when the old adage of quality, not quantity comes into play. Choose your friends and heroes wisely because they are the ones you turn to when you need help.

Mitra-labha teaches life lessons on how to make allies and friends who stand by you, with an emphasis on teamwork and mutual support which can overcome all problems.

Mitra Labha
The Gaining of Friends

2.1 The Agile Mouse

The sage had never seen a mouse jump so high to steal food! It was an amazing feat that could put even cats and dogs to shame. For weeks the sage had been trying to protect his bowl of food from the aggressive mouse, but he was yet to find success. The sage lived in a temple, and the food he procured, he distributed to other poor workers who kept the temple clean. But the mouse had come from nowhere and disturbed his routine.

"I have tried everything to save my food from the mouse, but that mouse is so resourceful. He can jump and attack the bowl however high it is. Even now as I talk to you, I have to continuously hit the bowl with a stick to scare the mouse away. I cannot even focus on my spiritual practice," confided the sage to a visitor in the temple.

The wise visitor suggested, "The mouse is so active, so agile; there has to be some reason behind it. The only possible reason for his overzealous actions is that he has a reservoir of surplus food. This is what gives him confidence to jump extraordinarily high. He knows he has nothing to lose and has no fear."

They decided to track the mouse and find his storehouse. The tracks led them to the hole of the mouse. On digging a bit, they found a large pile of food he had safely stacked away. They took it away to see what happens.

When the mouse found his food stack missing, he became dejected. He went in search of more food but he no longer felt the same zeal and confidence. When he tried to reach the high bowl of food, he could not save himself from the sage's stick and he fell on the floor. Heartbroken, he decided to leave the temple and find another home.

Lesson

Every problem can be solved by going to the root of it.

2.2 The Mice Save the Elephants

It was a golden era for the mice. Their population was growing steadily with comfortable housing and ample food. What was a disaster for the humans had been a blessing for the mice. An earthquake had destroyed a village and all the villagers had abandoned the village and fled to safety. The mice occupied the entire village without the fear of being trapped or killed by the cruel humans.

Although life was good, there was one thing that troubled them. A large lake nearby was frequented by a herd of elephants for bathing and frolicking. They marched through the village to reach the lake and in the process trampled hundreds of mice without care. This was a daily occurrence. The king of mice was under pressure to find a solution before the situation escalated. He thought he would try a peace proposal first.

He approached the king of elephants and narrated his woes to him, "O mighty sir, your herd of elephants unknowingly kills hundreds of mice daily as it walks back and forth to the lake. On compassionate grounds, can you please change your path to the lake? We shall never forget this kindness, and will return the favour whenever you need help."

The elephant king burst into laughter. How could the tiny insignificant mice help the mighty herd of elephants? But he did not want to hurt any living being unnecessarily. He said, "We are extremely sorry for being the cause of death of your near and dear ones. Although we don't need any favours from you, we will stop passing through your village. Do not worry any more, o' king of mice."

Thanking the magnanimous elephant king, the king of mice returned to his village happily. Just a few days had passed when a messenger came bearing a message from the elephant king.

The elephant herd had been trapped in a net set up by an elephant-hunter. They struggled to set

themselves free but the net was too strong for them. The elephant king had then remembered the promise given by the king of mice and had sent for his help. The messenger pleaded the mice to help them urgently.

The king of mice summoned all the mice and the rescue army rushed to the spot. Hundreds of mice nibbled on the net and cut it apart at a great speed. The elephants were free and grateful to the mice for helping them on time.

Lesson

Do not be fooled by size. What matters is quality, not quantity.

2.3 The Seed Story

"When we ourselves are so poor, what sense does it make to give charity to others?" The poor Brahmin's wife argued with her frail but determined husband. He always believed in the power of giving. He believed that when one gives, he also receives. But she thought otherwise. In her opinion, receiving always made more sense than giving. In fact, she went out of her way to outsmart others to her advantage.

The Brahmin was going to the city on a very auspicious day, for a festival that was celebrated with much pomp in the city. He knew that people would be in a charitable mood that day. He convinced his wife that if he travelled to the city, he would surely collect enough alms to last them for a long time. But he also felt that they should invite some poorer Brahmin and feed him something on this auspicious occasion. That was where the argument had begun. His wife was reluctant. Finally, they agreed that she would cook a very simple dish from sesame seeds.

The kind Brahmin left the next morning. The lady busied herself in cleaning the husk of the sesame seeds and allowed it to dry in the sun. While she was attending to her household chores, a dog came by and dirtied the dried seeds. When she realised what had happened, she panicked. She knew that she had very little time left before the guest arrived. Not wanting to waste the contaminated seeds but at the same time not wanting to make a dish out of them, she began to think of a way out.

She walked up to her neighbour and offered her the unhusked seeds in exchange for seeds that had husk. The neighbour, unable to comprehend why she was doing that, thought it was a good exchange. She bartered her good husky seeds with the contaminated unhusked seeds.

The Brahmin's wife was delighted but as they were about to make the exchange, the son of the lady stepped in. He asked a very simple question that planted a seed of doubt in his mother's mind.

"Why would someone who has seeds that are clean exchange them for unhusked seeds? There must be some reason she doesn't want to disclose. Anyone who acts extra kindly in this world surely has a hidden agenda behind it. Every lucrative offer has hidden loopholes."

The mother saw logic in his words and refused to part with her fresh stock. The Brahmin's wife returned home with a heavy heart.

Lesson
If anyone offers something that is too good to be true, think twice before you latch on to that offer.

2.4 The Unusual Conversation

"This place is good for nothing! No one values quality. Look at the way the other tailors are prospering. Their garments are inferior to mine. But they are making huge profits. People here just don't understand the value of good quality. I shouldn't be here," Somilaka, the tailor, was lamenting his failure to his wife.

He had been contemplating moving to another city to try his luck. Until today he had been reluctant to do so because he knew that his wife wouldn't agree. But today he was determined. He had faced the greatest financial loss after investing a large amount into buying a high

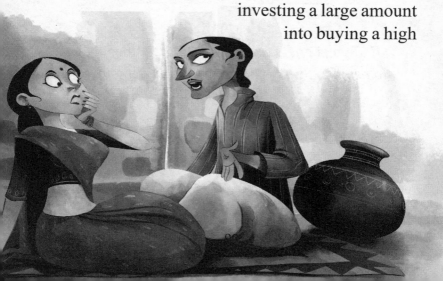

quality material that no one in the market had. Unfortunately, no one in the city had appreciated his superior product. He had had enough and decided to leave the very next morning to try his luck in another city.

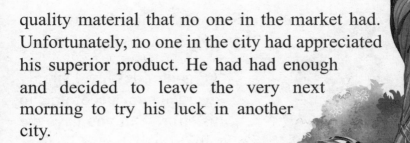

Though his wife didn't want him to leave, Somilaka left anyway. Lady luck favoured him, and in a matter of three years he had become rich and famous for his superior clothing. When he had managed to save about 300 gold coins, he decided to wind up and return to his family.

On his way, he decided to rest under a tree in the middle of a forest. Suddenly he heard two voices whispering.

"O' god of action, why did you allow this tailor to earn so much wealth? He doesn't deserve it according to his destiny," said the voice of destiny.

"O' god of destiny, I simply awarded him according to his effort. But you have the authority to decide whether you want him to retain that wealth or not," said the voice of action.

The unusual conversation triggered fear in his heart and he dug his hands into his bag to check on his wealth. To his dismay, the 300 gold coins were missing! His hard-earned wealth was gone. Utterly sad, he couldn't proceed further but returned to the city. In a year, he again saved about 500 gold coins with his intelligence and hard work. Again he started towards home triumphantly. On his way, he once again heard the two voices. The voice of destiny was once again chastising the voice of action for allowing him to earn so much. The voice of action reiterated that he was awarded according to his effort but whether he could retain the wealth or not was the choice of the god of destiny.

With great fear he looked through the bag and found the money missing. This was too unbearable. Miserable that he was unable to provide for his family, he decided to end his life. Weaving a strong rope by tying grass together, he tied the rope to a banyan tree and was about to place a noose around his neck when he heard a familiar voice.

"I am the god of destiny. I am the one who has taken away all the gold coins from you since you don't need that much for your livelihood.

But I am very happy with you, considering your effort. I would like to offer you a boon. Please ask me for anything."

Somilaka was thrilled! He said, "Gold coins! Lots of gold coins. That's all I ask for."

The god of destiny tried to explain to him that he was not destined to earn more than what he needed for a living. But Somilaka was adamant and would not take "no" for an answer. On seeing his stubbornness, the god of destiny agreed to give him wealth. But he had a condition. He wanted him to go back to the city and visit two merchants. After studying their behaviour, he wanted Somilaka to decide which type of wealth he wanted.

Accordingly, the next evening he reached the house of a very rich merchant and sought shelter. Unhesitatingly the merchant provided him food and shelter for the night but in the most insulting manner. Having no choice, Somilaka spent the night there. He heard the two voices conversing once again.

The god of destiny spoke first, "O' god of action, you shouldn't have allowed the merchant to provide food and shelter to him. He doesn't deserve it as he forced himself there as an unwanted guest."

The god of action replied, "O' god of destiny, the tailor needed shelter for the night but the merchant gave it to him in a very miserly manner. You decide what should be their destiny."

Leaving that merchant's house, Somilaka travelled once again. The next night he took shelter in another merchant's house. Though not as rich, the second merchant was much more hospitable. He, in fact, arranged for a lavish dinner and went out of his way to serve his unexpected guest. That night he heard the two voices speak again. Though the god of destiny was still upset with the god of action for providing accommodation to the unwanted guest, the god of action was happy with the attitude of the second merchant for going out of his way to serve his guest. As usual, action left the consequence to destiny.

The next morning, the tailor saw the king's people bring a huge amount of wealth to the second merchant's house. Somilaka realised that destiny had chosen to reward him for his kindness. With this experience, he set out once again to meet the god of destiny who was waiting to know what wealth Somilaka would settle for.

Somilaka had learnt that though the first merchant was very rich, he was miserly. That wealth had made him selfish and thus he couldn't enjoy life for the fear of losing his wealth. The second merchant, though he wasn't rich, lived a life of joy, sharing whatever he had with others, and thus was satisfied. Somilaka chose to live a life like the second merchant. With a little wealth but a satisfied life.

Destiny then smiled at him and continued smiling at him for the rest of his life.

Lesson

When you put in efforts, you will get results. But whether you can retain those results will depend on your attitude towards life and other people.

Kaakah and Ulukah are Sanskrit words for crow and owl respectively. Crows represent the good, being creatures of the day. While owls represent the strong evil forces, being creatures of the night. Life is a battle of good versus evil, light versus darkness. The battle between good and evil is not just a battle of physical might but more a battle of wits. So what we learn from these stories is that battles can be won by swords of wit rather than swords of might.

Kakolukiyam is about war and peace; it is about being good in behaviour and not just good in speech, and discriminating the good from the bad.

Kakolukiyam

Of Crows and Owls

3.1 The Opinionated Crow

The jungle was reverberating with the sounds of drums and conches. The entire bird fraternity had gathered to coronate the owl as the king of the birds. It was a moment of pride as they had finally found a king who was concerned about their welfare. All birds except the crow were present for the meeting and had unanimously decided that the owl was a good choice. He could see during night when the other birds were helpless. He would surely make a powerful king!

Soon the crow flew in and asked what the celebration was all about. The birds explained – Garuda, their present king, was too busy with his duties to bother about them. Given his indifference, it made sense to appoint another king who could be more hands on. So they had settled for the mighty owl!

The crow disapproved of their choice and presented his argument, "The owl is blind during the day! His crooked nose  gives him a cruel appearance. We have such beautiful birds – the peacock, the swan, the nightingale who are much more eligible. And what is the advantage of having the owl as king? The mere mention of Garuda is enough to scare away our enemies. We don't need a new king. Please stop this coronation, friends."

The birds considered his words. His logic made sense. They said, "Let's postpone this decision and meet again." All of them flew away.

The owl overheard the entire conversation. "You evil crow," he cried, "Have I ever harmed you? Why did you spoil my life?" and he cursed the crow. "From today, owls and crows will never be friends. They will be lifelong enemies."

The crow hung his head in sorrow. He had created a long lasting enmity between two groups of birds by his thoughtless words.

Lesson
Using words that hurt can have a long term effect and bring trouble for us.

3.2 Hares versus Elephants

"Ah, water! Sweet water!" the jubilant elephants squealed and jigged when they saw the vast expanse of crystal clear water. Their knowledgeable king had led them here to quench their thirst. The jungle was experiencing a severe drought and they had been walking for days together. The search ended as they jumped into the lake with sheer delight.

Rushing to the water, they trampled on the soft earth surrounding the lake which was home to many a hare. Numerous hares were crushed to

death and many more were injured. The surviving hares fled fast to save their lives. Once the elephants had departed, they gathered to discuss the misfortune that had befallen them.

The question was, should they run from there to save their lives or stay back and face death? The vote was divided. One hare stood up to speak, "Why should we leave our ancestral home? Let's scare the elephants so they don't come back here. Here's my plan…"

"Go back, go back! The moon god is angry with you. Do not step ahead!" the hare shouted at the elephants. Surprised, the king of elephants asked the hare why the moon god was angry.

"This lake belongs to the moon god and I'm his messenger. He is angry because you killed many hares yesterday who were under his protection. Now if you enter the lake, he will destroy you."

"We do not want to anger the moon god," said the elephant king, "But we would like to apologise to him. Can you take us to him?"

The clever hare took them to the lake and showed them the reflection of the moon. He said, "The moon god is meditating, do not disturb him."

The elephants bowed to him and retreated respectfully. The herd left without a word. And the hares lived happily without any more disturbance.

Lesson

The winners in life are not those who are physically strong but those who are mentally strong.

3.3 The Bird that Lost its Home

The little partridge was highly disturbed. Her home was gone. A little rabbit had occupied it while she was away for a few days. The partridge called out to her friend who stayed on a high branch on the same tree. Her friend couldn't do anything but shrug her shoulders. They were no match for the rabbit. In fact, many times, her friend had told her to take up a place on top of the tree rather than settling into a hole at the roots of the tree. No bird ever made its nest at the bottom of a tree, for obvious reasons! But the little partridge was adamant and wanted a different setting for her special home. Now she was facing the consequence of her choice.

As the little partridge argued back and forth with the rabbit to vacate her home, she realised that this was not going to work. The little partridge proposed to the rabbit to bring in a wise person who understood the code of ethics, to decide who should actually be the rightful occupant of that hole. The rabbit immediately agreed to have a mediator settle the dispute. Now the only question was: who could that be?

As the rabbit and the partridge argued, there was a hungry, wild cat loitering around searching for an easy prey. He happened to overhear the conversation between the two fighting parties. Suddenly he felt that he had hit a jackpot. Two, not one!

The rabbit and the partridge walked around looking for someone who would be an ideal mediator. Someone who was not only wise but also trustworthy. That's when they spotted the wild cat standing on his hind legs, eyes closed in a meditative pose, holding the holy kusa grass in his paws. Just looking at him they felt peaceful. He radiated holiness. As soon as the partridge spotted the saintly personality, she turned towards the rabbit and pointed in his direction. The rabbit was impressed too.

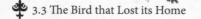

The two walked up to the saint who was in the midst of a meditative trance. Not forgetting that he was ultimately a tomcat, a natural predator for both the rabbit and the partridge, they stood at a good distance. The partridge spoke up, sharing her complete story with the saintly cat.

"O' sister partridge, I am hard of hearing. As I am getting older, my hearing capacity is decreasing steadily. Please come closer and share your woes. Don't worry about me being a cat. I'm not a regular cat anymore. I have developed higher saintly qualities that have convinced me about the frailties of living a life of violence. If I don't even kill mosquitoes and ticks that bite me, then why must you fear me?"

That convinced the partridge and the rabbit, who sat next to the grinning cat to explain the details of their conflict. The next moment the cat leaped

on them and the two were fighting not with each other but with their common enemy.

Lesson

Beware of those who claim to be good.
Goodness is not spoken about but shown
in action.

3.4 A Goat Demon

One rainy day, Mitra Sharma was walking from one village to another, carrying a goat on his shoulders. Since the distance was considerable and he needed to reach without any delay, he wanted to have full control over the goat and thus had decided that the best course of action would be to carry it on his shoulders. Unknown to him, he was being watched by a gang of three crooks who had their eyes on the goat.

As Sharma walked hurriedly, one of the crooks walked past him, laughing loudly and pointing in his direction. Unable to control himself, he began rolling on the ground with laughter. Finally, he said, "Why would any sane man carry a street dog on his shoulders like that? Are you out of your mind?"

Mitra Sharma got annoyed. How could this man not know the difference between

a dog and a goat? Deciding to ignore the foolishness, he walked away. A little distance away another man crossed his way. Initially that man seemed lost in thought, but suddenly a smile appeared on his face. That smile turned into a chuckle and then into roaring laughter. This was getting annoying now.

"Why would any sane man carry a dead calf on his shoulders like that? Are you out of your mind?" This comment drove Mitra Sharma mad with anger. He burst out, "Don't you know the difference between a goat and a calf? And it's not dead, it's very much alive. Can't you see?"

That man continued laughing, totally ignoring Mitra's anger. Mitra continued his journey till he came across a third man who was also roaring with laughter. "Why would any sane man carry a donkey on his shoulders like that? Are you out of your mind?"

This was too much. How could three people be wrong? Now a thought began to take shape in Mitra Sharma's head which changed into fear and then became paranoia. What if this was not a goat but rather a shape-shifting demon that he was carrying?

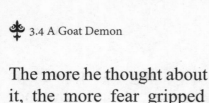

The more he thought about it, the more fear gripped him. All kinds of images of the demon who was seated on his shoulders began to flash in his mind. He suddenly dropped the goat. Without even turning behind to see what he had dropped, he ran away in great fear and haste.

The three crooks were now laughing at the foolishness of the man who had believed them. They took away the goat and kept it for themselves.

Lesson

When a lie is spoken enough times, it appears to be truer than truth itself.

3.5 The Transformation of a Cruel Hunter

He shivered as much with fear as he did with cold as the chilling wind whipped around him. The heavy downpour, thundering and lightening had scared even a hard-hearted hunter like him. Known as Yama, his friends and relatives had deserted him because of his cruel ways. Today, ironically, he was running helter-skelter looking for shelter from nature's fury!

The tree he stood under was the home of the female dove he had captured just before the storm. He still had her captive in a cage. The female dove heard the voice of her companion praying for her safety and called out to him. "Oh my love, I am right here under the tree, caught by a hunter. But don't feel sorry for me. My suffering is because of my own past deeds. We have heard the sages say many times that diseases and disasters are a result of one's own past karmas. So do not lament or carry hate for the hunter. He is not to be blamed. Treat him like your guest because he has taken shelter under your house. He is cold and hungry so take good care of him."

The male dove was very touched by the female dove's noble thoughts. He drew inspiration from her and flew down to the hunter. He said, "Welcome to my abode, my friend. Is there anything I can do for you?"

The hunter was relieved to hear a kind voice. He said, "Can you help me get warm? I will soon die of the cold."

The dove collected some dry leaves and with a burning coal he lit a fire. He said, "Here's a fire to keep you warm. I also offer myself, please satisfy your hunger by making a meal out of me."

The dove stepped into the fire and died instantly. The hunter was amazed at the selflessness of the bird. If a bird could have such high values, then why couldn't he? He felt ashamed of himself. He thought, "This bird has taught me a big lesson on sacrifice. I have lived a wicked life and will surely go to hell. But from today, I will change my ways and lead a sin-free life."

He released the female dove and threw away the cage. The female dove was heartbroken to learn that her beloved companion had sacrificed himself. She too rushed into the fire and killed herself. Both the doves met in heaven where they found spiritual bliss. Whereas the hunter, transformed by the doves, lived the life of a sage. One day the forest caught fire and the hunter willingly gave up his life in the fire as penance for his past deeds. Having burnt his sins, he too found his way to the higher planets.

Lesson

*Setting an example by self-sacrifice inspires
others to become better.*

3.6 The Brahmin and the Gold Coins

Was he really seeing a gold coin or were his eyes playing tricks? The poor Brahmin blinked in amazement as he saw a shiny gold coin in the plate he had used to offer milk to a cobra. He had never expected to see or touch a gold coin in his life!

Just one day ago he had spotted a cobra in his field. Considering it to be a representative of God, he had worshipped it, asking for prosperity because however hard he tilled his farm, there was no yield.

And the cobra had reciprocated. He pocketed the gold coin as the cobra's blessing. Now everyday he offered milk and found a gold coin. This continued for many days and the Brahmin grew in wealth. One day, in his absence, he instructed his son to offer milk to the cobra and keep the blessing he got in return.

When the Brahmin's son saw the gold coin, he thought there must be many more in the cobra's burrow. "Why not kill the cobra and gather all the wealth at one go?" he thought. With this intention, he waited for the cobra to emerge and hit him with a stick. The cobra fought back and bit the boy. The boy died while the cobra survived.

The Brahmin's relatives advised him to take revenge but the Brahmin knew it was not the cobra who was at fault. He went to the same spot to offer milk and prayers. The cobra emerged and confronted the Brahmin, "All you care about is wealth. Your son is dead but you still come here for the gold coin. His greed killed him but you have still not learnt a lesson. I have no affection left for you, my heart is broken. Go away and never come back." The cobra gave the Brahmin a parting gift, a big sparkling diamond.

The Brahmin walked back home, lamenting the loss of both, his son as well as the blessings of the cobra.

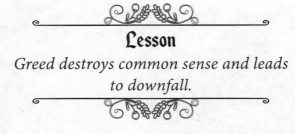

Lesson

Greed destroys common sense and leads to downfall.

3.7 The Helpful Thief

Kamatura was an old man now. After he lost his wife, he felt very lonely and wanted someone who would love him. Inspired by his friends, he decided to marry once again at his ripe old age. He convinced a poor man to give him his daughter in marriage and offered him a huge sum of money in return. The marriage took place soon. Unfortunately, the young girl was not happy with the marriage and had agreed only due to the pressure of her parents.

After the marriage, she flatly refused to comply with her husband in any way. Though Kamatura showered her with loads of gifts and love, she would not reciprocate. She even chose to sleep on a separate cot placed at the far end of the room, away from her husband's cot.

One night as they were fast asleep, a thief entered the house. As he stealthily moved around the house, his faint footsteps disturbed the wife's sleep. When she sensed that there was someone in the house, a great fear developed in her heart and she ran to her husband's bed and embraced him tightly. The sudden embrace of his wife woke the happy husband. This was a miracle.

But he was not a fool; he realized she had only done it out of fear. And then he realized that there was a thief in the house. Out of sheer joy, he spoke loudly to the lurking thief.

"O thief, you are my best friend. You will never know how much you have helped me unknowingly. You have offered me the greatest wealth I treasure, the embrace of my wife. You may take anything you like from my house with no fear of being caught."

Lesson

Many a time, our worst enemy could be our best friend.

3.8 The Failed Partnership

The thief's eyes sparkled as he glanced at his next target. From the moment he set his eyes on the two beautiful fat calves, he decided that he had to steal them. They would surely fetch him a good sum when sold.

He planned the theft for the same night. Surely, in the middle of the night, the Brahmin who owned the calves would be snoring away. As planned, he began to walk towards the village from the forest where he lived. Suddenly a fierce monster appeared in his path. The thief trembled in fear. The monster asked for his identity, warning him that he hated liars. The thief immediately revealed his plan for the night. Somehow he managed to strike a deal with the monster. The deal was that they would raid the house together. While the thief stole the calves, the monster would eat the Brahmin. Thus, both their ends would be achieved in one place.

As soon as they reached there, the demon

entered the house and the thief entered the courtyard. Suddenly the thief realised something. He stopped the monster from entering the house. He demanded that the monster enter the house only after he had stolen the calves, else the Brahmin may wake up and catch him stealing. The monster disagreed. He said that, in fact, it should be the other way round. If the thief stole the calves, they would undoubtedly begin mooing, then the Brahmin may escape the monster's clutches.

Soon they were intensely arguing with each other. The noise woke the Brahmin up and he came out of the house. The two began to complain against each other to the Brahmin. The Brahmin sensed the situation and began to chant mantras to drive away the monster. He then took a stick and drove away the thief too.

Lesson
When two people fight, a third always benefits.

121

3.9 The Princess Saves the Prince

The son of king Devashakti had everything that money could buy. The young prince was surrounded by opulence. But what money could not buy him was physical strength and good health. The boy was losing weight on a daily basis and, as a result, was getting weaker and weaker. He was afflicted by a strange condition – he had a snake in his stomach. No medicine had worked. The best of the physicians in the kingdom had given up hope, saying it was incurable.

King Devashakti felt helpless and hopeless when he saw his son so weakened and withered. How would he rule the kingdom? The young boy too felt his father's frustration and it troubled him a lot. To make things easier for his father, one night, he silently walked out of the palace never to return again.

He went to another kingdom where he would not be recognised and made his base in a temple. The king of that kingdom had two lovely daughters, very cultured and well-mannered. One would take his blessings every day and say, "Your blessings bring me all the possible happiness, my dear father." While the other would say, "One gets whatever one is destined to get as per the law of karma."

Although the king loved both his daughters, he would get upset by his second daughter's words. One day he told his minister, "I will prove to her how wrong she is. Take her away and get her married to the first boy you can find!"

As was her destiny, the first boy the minister found was the young prince in the temple. The two were married off. The princess was happy and content with her husband. They decided to travel to another kingdom and make a home for themselves. On the way, the weak prince wanted to rest. The princess left him sleeping to arrange for some food. When she returned, she saw the most surprising sight of her life! A snake was slithering out of her husband's mouth! She rubbed her eyes. Was she imagining this? No, the snake was very real, and was having a conversation with another snake that had emerged from an anthill.

The other snake said, "Why do you live in this boy's stomach even now? What do you achieve by torturing him? The day he drinks a cumin and mustard flavoured soup, you will die. You should find a better life."

The snake replied, "What do you achieve by living in this small anthill and guarding two pots of gold? Pouring hot water with coconut oil will kill you instantly. Go somewhere else, I say."

Thus the two snakes argued and then went back to their shelters again. The clever princess knew what she had to do. She fed her husband cumin and mustard flavoured soup and she poured hot water and coconut oil over the anthill. She collected the two pots of gold and her husband started to recover and gain his health again. There were no obstacles in their happiness now.

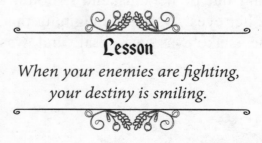

Lesson
*When your enemies are fighting,
your destiny is smiling.*

3.10 The Guru and the Mouse

While bathing and praying in the sacred waters of river Ganga, Guru Yadnyavalkya was rudely awakened from his meditation. A mouse had dropped down from the sky into his open palms. Startled, he looked up. He saw a hawk circling overhead, eyeing its prey that had slipped out of its claws. How could he let the hawk capture the mouse? Feeling compassion for the mouse, he transformed the female mouse into a small girl and brought her to his hut. His wife readily accepted her as the daughter she had always yearned for.

The girl grew up and became wise and knowledgeable under the wings of her learned father. Soon the proud parents thought it was time to get her married. The Guru thought hard about a suitable match as she was a special child who deserved a special husband.

No one could be more apt than the Sun God, who was the source of strength for the entire universe. He concentrated on his mystical powers and summoned the Sun God and said, "My daughter is special. I wish to marry her to you, if she agrees."

But the daughter said, "Oh father, the sun is too fiery and hot-tempered. I cannot live with him."

The father was disappointed with his daughter's refusal. Who could be better than the Sun God? But the Sun God suggested that the Guru ask the King of Clouds to marry her as only he had the capacity to cover the sun. He was therefore the superior choice. The Guru readily agreed and summoned the King of Clouds. He said, "My daughter is special. I wish to marry her to you, if she agrees."

However, his daughter said, "Dear father, the King of Clouds is dark and wet. Please find someone else."

The Guru was once again disheartened but the King of Clouds suggested he seek the hand of the Lord of Winds, who had the power to blow the clouds away. The Lord of Winds was summoned but the girl said, "No, father, I will never be able to keep up with the Lord of Winds, he is too fast and restless."

The Guru felt utterly dejected but the Lord of Winds thought the King of Mountains would be a good choice because only he could stop the wind from blowing. When the King of Mountains appeared, the girl shook her head. "He is too hard and rigid. Not my kind at all."

The poor father was ready to give up but the mountain suggested that the perfect choice would be the King of Mice as he was far superior and could make holes even in a mountain. No harm in trying, thought the Guru. He called upon the King of Mice and introduced him to his daughter. The daughter smiled shyly and approved of the match. The Guru then transformed the girl into a beautiful female mouse so she could live a happy married life.

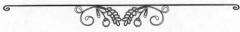

Lesson

What is inborn remains ingrained
and it can never change.

3.11 The Golden Stool

The hunter was exhausted after a whole day's hunt which had resulted in nothing at all. This was the third consecutive day that he couldn't lay his hands on any animal or bird. Just as he sat and rested his tired back against a huge tree trunk, there was a splash one inch away. What does one expect when they sit under a tree in the evening? Thanking destiny that the bird hadn't dropped on his head, he was about to close his eyes. Just then, from the corner of his eye, he saw something shimmer.

He opened his eyes and glanced at the bird's droppings. Pure gold! He couldn't believe his eyes. He rubbed them and saw again. Yes, it was pure gold! The droppings, as soon as they touched the earth, had turned into gold. He was amazed at the possibility of a bird whose droppings turned into gold. Wanting to trap the amazing bird, he stood up. All his exhaustion was gone. In a few minutes he managed to set up an irresistible trap for the bird.

Lo and behold, the magical bird was trapped. Though it looked like an ordinary bird, every dropping it laid turned into gold. The hunter was thrilled thinking about the fortune he was about to make with this bird. Another thought suddenly flashed across his mind. If he sold this gold in the market regularly, it would be hard to explain the source, and sooner or later the king's tax collectors would come knocking at his door. Instead, it would be wiser to sell the bird to the king itself for a hefty sum of money.

When the hunter presented the magical bird to the king, the king was excited. Ordering his people to pay the hunter a handsome reward, the king began to admire the bird. As soon as the hunter left, the ministers planted seeds of doubt in the king's mind. They said that the hunter had probably fooled the king. How could an ordinary looking bird have such magical features?

When the king was provoked enough, he ordered the guards to arrest the hunter and free the bird.

As soon as the bird was freed from its cage, it flew to a nearby tree and dropped. The droppings immediately turned into gold. Everyone was shocked at the sight. The king ordered his guards to catch the bird. Of course, the bird had learnt its lesson and never got trapped again.

Lesson

Before you conclude that something is impossible, assume that it is possible and verify.

3.12 The Talking Cave

The hungry lion walked all around the jungle with absolutely no hope. Of late the animals had become too smart and hunting was becoming more and more difficult. Wherever he went, news of his arrival would reach before him and the animals would disappear. As he was wandering about in sorrow, he came across a huge cave.

Surely there must be a lot of animals residing in such a big cave. He decided to explore the cave. Unfortunately, it was empty. But he was sure that some animal would return by dusk to sleep there. He waited patiently inside the cave for his dinner to walk in. Meanwhile, a clever jackal who resided in the cave returned home. Just as he was about to step into the cave, he noticed the footprints of a lion entering the cave but not exiting the cave. He was scared. He didn't want to die, but he also didn't want to abandon his home without confirming the danger.

Walking up to the edge of the cave, he shouted with great confidence, "O' cave, I have returned. Can I come in?"

The lion, who was waiting inside for its prey, was surprised at this call. He didn't know what to do. He decided to wait. The jackal continued shouting, "O' cave, have you forgotten our understanding of all these years? You promised  to always respond to my calls. If you do not respond, I will be forced to find some other cave."

The lion panicked, not wanting to lose his meal. It felt that the cave was not answering because of his presence. He decided to invite the jackal on behalf of the cave. In a thunderous voice, the lion spoke. "O' jackal, please enter. It's absolutely safe for you to enter."

The jackal, of course, never ever entered the cave that echoed terribly with the lion's booming voice.

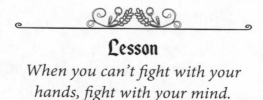

Lesson

When you can't fight with your hands, fight with your mind.

3.13 The Joyride

The frogs were surprised at the unusual sight. They had never seen the snake inactive. Usually the snake came to the pond to hunt for frogs. But today, he lay motionless on the bank of the pond, uninterested in them. They waited in anticipation, alert that they may have to run for their life. But strangely, the snake continued to be indifferent to them.

Unable to control his curiosity, one of the frogs went closer and asked, "Why are you not catching frogs today, as is your nature?"

The snake replied, "I have been cursed, O' frog. Yesterday I bit a Brahmin's son and the Brahmin cursed me." The snake broke into sobs and continued, "He said that from now on, I will not be able to catch a frog, instead I have to serve the race of frogs and eat whatever they give me. So I'm here, waiting to be of any service to you. I can take you for a ride on my back if you like."

Word was sent to the king of frogs and the royal entourage came to meet the snake. They found the snake to be genuine and the king thought he should show the courage to ride on his back first. The ride was the most enjoyable thing he had done in his life. One by one the ministers and other frogs rode on the snake's back. The snake entertained them thoroughly by crawling in different ways, sometimes slow, sometimes fast, sometimes zig zag and sometimes in the air. The frogs had the time of their lives.

The snake was thrilled to have executed half his plan successfully. Being old, he was unable to hunt for his food and this was his plan to get food easily. The next day would see the second half of his plan unfold.

The next day he appeared at the pond again to serve the frogs. The king of frogs wanted to start his day with a ride. He noticed that the snake was very slow and dull that day. The snake said, "Since I can't hunt myself, I have not eaten in many days. I feel too weak to move fast."

The king of frogs consulted his ministers. If they didn't feed him, none of them would get a ride.

So they decided to give the snake one frog a day in exchange for the ride. This is exactly what the old snake had planned – free meals without any effort. In a short time, he became strong and healthy, with a daily diet of frogs.

No one realised the snake's motive and slowly the number of frogs in the pond began to shrink till only a handful were remaining.

He became so strong that when other snakes came to enquire about the unusual joyrides, he would eat them too. When he had eaten all the frogs, he ate the ministers and finally the king too.

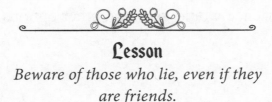

Lesson

Beware of those who lie, even if they are friends.

3.14 Checkmated by the Crows

There was a call for an urgent meeting to discuss a matter of life and death. Meghavrana, the king of crows, had summoned his council of ministers regarding the neighbouring owls who were creating a terror for the crow clan. They took advantage of their night vision to aggressively attack and kill the crows. He asked his five learned men for their advice.

All five suggested making peace with the enemy as they did not have the resources to fight them. The king, however, was not convinced. He turned to Sthirajeevi, an old minister who had served his father. Maybe his experience would give him other options.

The wise crow said, "The ministers' suggestion falls under Nitishastra, which is the right thing to do under ordinary circumstances. But this is no ordinary situation. The owls will not be interested in signing a peace treaty. We have to use our guile. I suggest we send a spy to find their weakness…" and he outlined his idea to the king. The king immediately swung into action.

As per the plan, Meghavrana pounced upon Sthirajeevi, injured him till he bled and threw him down the banyan tree. Then the entire crow clan left the banyan tree and flew to Rshyamukan mountain and waited for the plan to unfold.

At night, the owls attacked the banyan tree, but to their surprise not a single crow was found. Arimardana, the king of owls, saw Sthirajeevi and captured him and brought him back to their cave. Although his ministers advised him to kill Sthirajeevi, Arimardana thought Sthirajeevi could lead them to the crows' new hideout. He fed him well and nursed him back to health. Sthirajeevi requested permission to build a nest at the entrance of the cave. Slowly, he managed to gather a whole bunch of twigs at the entrance, pretending to make a nest.

At noon, while the owls were all sleeping, he flew to the Rshyamukan mountain and signalled to the crows to follow him with burning wood in their beaks. Hordes of crows swooped on the enemy cave and dropped the burning wood on the twigs strategically placed at the entrance. Sthirajeevi had been constructing a funeral pyre for them. The twigs soon caught fire and the smoke and heat made it impossible for the owls to escape from the cave and save their lives.

The crows could breathe in peace again thanks to their fearless king and the old minister.

Lesson
Inviting your enemy home is as good as inviting trouble for yourself.

Have you ever wished you were someone else or that you didn't have to do certain things? Then here are stories that will help you avoid giving in to peer pressure and getting carried away by shrewd people with wrong intentions. With examples of what one should avoid in life, these stories teach us what to watch out for and the consequences of one's actions.

The theme of Labdhpranasam is the loss of gains. It teaches you how not to lose what you already have, to follow rules and regulations of the society, to stay away from trouble and, to be genuine without trying to be what you are not.

Labdhapranasam

Loss of Gains

4.1 The Monkey Heart

There was a monkey named Raktamukha who loved blackberries. And why wouldn't he? After all, he lived on the biggest blackberry tree in the area. All day he would eat berries and play with his friends. One day, after the monkey had eaten a sumptuous meal of berries, he glanced below and saw a strange-looking animal outstretched at the roots of the tree.

It was a crocodile named Karalamukha. After a long swim in the river, the tired croc was resting under the shade of the tree. Calling out to him, the happy monkey welcomed him to his house. Since he was a guest, he had to be welcomed in the best possible way. The monkey couldn't think of a better way than offering him berries. Plucking a huge amount of berries, the monkey

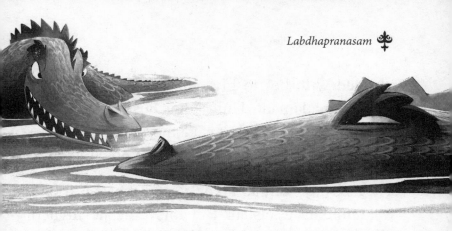

dropped them into the open mouth of the croc. Karalamukha was thrilled tasting the sweet blackberries. He loved them!

After spending the whole day together, discussing many things and eating berries, the crocodile left. He was happy to have found a good friend. Days passed and the two became best friends. Now the monkey not only fed his friend, but also began to send fruits for his family. When Karalamukha's wife ate the berries she was overjoyed. He had never seen her so happy. She said, "If these fruits are so sweet, then imagine how sweet the heart of the monkey will be who has been eating these for years. I want to taste his heart. Please get me the monkey's heart."

Karalamukha was shocked. How could he deceive his friend and bring his heart? He pleaded with her to give up her desire, but his wife was adamant. Unless her husband fulfilled her desire, she wouldn't eat a morsel of food. The despondent crocodile was left with no choice.

The next day, Karalamukha went to meet his friend Raktamukha as usual. But this time he invited him home to meet his wife. He told his friend that his wife loved the berries he sent so much that she desired to reciprocate by inviting him home. The monkey thanked him but expressed his inability to swim across the river to reach their home. Karalamukha proposed to carry him on his back across the river.

Soon the two friends were right in the middle of the river. The monkey had never been around so much water. He was really scared but confident that his friend would take care of him. When Karalamukha saw the fear in the monkey's eyes, he decided that it was safe to reveal his actual plan. When the monkey was told that the promised dinner was not for him but for his wife who was eager to dine on the monkey's heart, he laughed. The croc was surprised. Why would someone laugh about his own death?

The monkey then said, "If only you had told me that your wife desires to eat my heart, I would have got it along with me. I always keep my heart safely tucked away in the hollow of the blackberry tree. I carry it with me only when absolutely needed."

The crocodile froze. This was a disaster. He could imagine his wife's wrath if he went home without the monkey's heart. He panicked and asked his friend for a solution. The monkey was very reassuring and understanding. He said, "Don't worry, let's just return to the tree and bring along my heart."

The crocodile immediately turned around and swam back to the tree. As soon as they reached close by, the monkey jumped off the back of the crocodile and ran up the tree. Sitting on its topmost branch he caught his breath and thanked god for giving him the intelligence to save his life. The crocodile waited for a long time and finally called his friend. The monkey simply laughed.

He said, "You deceived me and I deceived you. Now we are even. Friendship should only be made with people who are trustworthy. I had actually given you my heart as a friend, but now you've lost it and will never get it back."

Lesson

Friendships should be made with people who are like minded.

4.2 The Poisonous Friendship

Living with your relatives can get really annoying. Especially if they are the irritating kind. That's what happened to Gangadatta, the king of frogs. He was surrounded by too many irritating relatives. Although he was the king, it was too much for him to handle. One day he decided to quit. He ran away from his own kingdom. But he couldn't forget the humiliation his relatives had subjected him to.

Wanting to take revenge for all the insults and frustration that his relatives had caused him, the king frog befriended a venomous cobra. Initially the cobra was too hesitant to connect with a frog as a friend. After all they were natural enemies. What was the possibility of a friendship between them? But

when the king frog promised him a daily quota of frogs to eat, the cobra agreed to his proposal.

The king frog took his new friend back to the well. He showed him a secret hole in the well from where he could have easy access to the frogs. The condition was that the cobra would only eat the frogs that were the king frog's enemies and not touch his friends. The cobra kept his promise and carefully avoided the king's friends while eating his enemies, one frog a day. A day came when all the enemies of the king frog were dead and gone. But the hunger of the cobra remained. And now it had increased! He had now gotten a taste for the frogs, and he refused to leave the king frog's well.

Having no other option left, the king frog had to allow him to eat his friends too. Soon, a day came when only his family remained. The cobra enjoyed feasting on the frogs mercilessly, until a day came when only the king frog remained.

In order to save his life, he assured the cobra that he would look for another well with a huge frog population. The cobra saw the big picture and realised that this proposition was better for

his future. So he decided to let the king frog go. The frog went away never to return. After a long wait, the cobra realised he had been duped. He sent a message through a lizard to the king frog conveying how much he missed his old friend.

When the king frog got the message, he smiled. The snake was clever, but the frog knew that a hungry being is the cruellest being. He was smart enough to never venture in that direction again. He had lost his relatives and friends, but he had gained a lesson he would never forget.

Lesson

Friendship with an enemy is worse than a fight with a relative.

149

4.3 The Potter and his Scar

"**W**hat a brave warrior he must be! Look at the impressive scar on his forehead," whispered the king to his minister. "He must have been injured while fighting a fierce battle," agreed the minister.

The king and his minister were looking for brave men to join their army and they immediately selected this man without any questions. In fact, they give him a place of honour amongst the best warriors in the kingdom.

The selected soldier, however, was always quiet. He was no soldier. He was Yudhishthira, a poor potter from the neighbouring kingdom in search of a living. This was not the time to tell the truth, he thought.

Soon a war broke out. The king summoned all the warriors and showered them with gifts. Amongst them was the poor potter. The king took him aside and asked him, "In which war did you get this deadly scar, my brave soldier?"

The potter could not hide the truth any longer. He said, "Forgive me, Your Highness, this scar is not from a war, neither am I a warrior. I am a poor potter. I tripped over some pots and injured my forehead. Having no money for medicines, the wound was left unattended and it became a big scar."

The king was highly embarrassed at his mistake. He told the potter to leave immediately. But the potter fell at his feet and said, "O king, please have mercy on me. Give me one chance to show my bravery on the battlefield. I will not let you down." He pleaded humbly.

The king, who had seen many battles, replied from his experience, "You may be brave, but on the battlefield you need the qualities of a warrior. You could get killed the very first day. Please return home and forget about being a warrior."

The potter knew the king was right and he returned home.

Lesson

If you align your work according to who you are, there is peace everywhere.

4.4 The Unusual Gift

"**H**ere's a gift for you, my dear," the lion presented his wife with an unusual bundle. It was a baby jackal he had found while hunting. The lioness looked at the innocent furry bundle and her heart melted. She agreed with the lion that they couldn't possibly kill him for food. He could grow up with her two little cubs. The more the merrier!

So the jackal became a part of the lion family, loved and cared for by doting parents. However, the children occasionally fought with each other, having very different natures and coming from different species. One day, while they were playing, a wild elephant rushed towards them. While the jackal wanted to flee for his life, the lion cubs wanted to face the elephant and fight him. But the young

153

jackal persuaded them saying, "He is our enemy and much stronger. Please let's just go home."

At home, the cubs made fun of the jackal and mocked him in front of their parents. The jackal felt upset and insulted. He confided in the lioness, "I am not a coward. In fact I saved their lives or the elephant would have killed us. If they don't understand this, I will kill them."

The lioness, although shocked, had expected this to happen sooner or later. She said, "My son, I know you are not a coward. But you are a jackal and they are lions. Although I have raised you as my son, it is now time for you to leave this family." She roared again, "Please go or I shall kill you myself!"

The jackal fled from there immediately to find the safety of his jackal family.

Lesson

*Knowing who you are and what your qualities
are can keep you away from trouble.*

4.5 The Rise of the Donkey

A poor washer man was worried about his donkey's health. He didn't have the means to feed him enough fodder. Though he made the donkey work hard, he didn't feed him well enough. One day he found something that ended his worries. It was a dead tiger. As soon as he saw the dead tiger in the forest, an idea struck him.

He brought the skin of the dead tiger home. That night, he covered his donkey with the skin of the tiger and let him into his neighbour's fields. The donkey grazed to his heart's content all night. When the washer man noticed that no one had detected the intrusion, he decided to try the trick again. Soon, the donkey was grazing in the neighbour's fields every night, dressed in the tiger skin.

Eventually the neighbours noticed the disturbance. But they dared not do anything to the tiger. Days passed in sheer joy for the donkey and his master. The donkey was well fed and the washer man saved so much fodder money.

One night, as the disguised donkey was grazing, he heard a familiar sound. Listening carefully he heard that pleasing sound again. Unmistakably, it was the sound of a female donkey. The donkey became so happy that it responded by braying loudly. When the neighbouring farmers heard the tiger braying like a donkey, they knew that they were being fooled.

Running towards the donkey dressed in a tiger's skin, they beat him up with all their might.

Lesson

Do not try to be what you are not meant to be.

4.6 The Foolish Camel

Making carts was not at all a profitable business. Ujjwalaka and his family were starving. Unable to make ends meet, he decided to leave the village and take up some odd job in another village. As they passed through the forest, they came across a pregnant camel that was writhing in pain. A caravan had passed by and abandoned the camel.

Ujjwalaka took great care of the pregnant camel and helped her deliver her baby smoothly. Since the camel had no home, he decided to take her along with the baby. Soon he fell in love with the baby camel and gave it a lot of attention.

When he began to sell the milk of the camel in the next village, he made good profit that easily maintained his family. In a few weeks, he even managed to buy another

camel. Very soon he owned a flock of camels. He would supply camel milk to the whole village. But despite having so many camels, the baby camel remained his favourite. He even put a belt with a tingling bell around his neck.

The baby camel soon became very proud of all the attention he received from his master. He shook the bell especially when many people were around, just to be the centre of attraction.

Every day the camels went to a nearby forest to graze. While all the other camels were obedient and followed instructions carefully, the baby camel was too proud and didn't care for any advice or instruction. Many a times, the other camels would prod it to hurry up and not lag

behind. But it took its own sweet time to eat and graze in the forest.

One day, as the other camels in the flock walked ahead, the baby camel lagged behind as usual. Even though everyone kept calling him, he walked slowly, ringing his bell to show off. A watchful lion waited for the others in the flock to distance themselves from the baby camel. Just when he was all alone, the lion jumped and attacked the baby camel.

Lesson
Pride is like an ear-plug that blocks good advice.

4.7 The Jackal's Strategy Code

Lady luck was smiling down on Mahachaturaka, the jackal. He had found a huge dead elephant which was all his to feast upon. Such a bounty came once in a lifetime. He thanked his stars and attacked the elephant with a voracious appetite. But he was utterly frustrated when, after many attempts, he was simply unable to tear the elephant's thick skin. He tried the front, the back, the sides, but in vain. How long, he despaired, before another animal came and snatched the elephant away from him?

Right then he saw a lion coming. The jackal bowed to him and said, "Dear king, I have hunted this elephant for you. Please accept this token of appreciation and eat it."

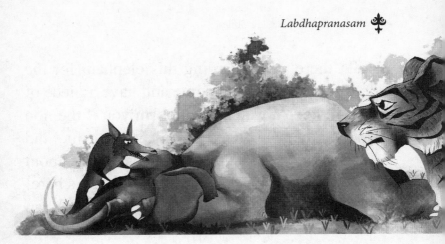

The lion was unimpressed. He said, "Thanks, but no thanks. I eat only what I kill."

The jackal heaved a sigh of relief but soon he saw a leopard approaching. Humility would not work with the leopard. He said to him, "Dear brother, there is danger here. I'm guarding this elephant that was hunted by the lion. If he sees you here, you will be in trouble." This was enough to scare the leopard, and he left faster than his legs could take him.

"Phew! That was a close call," sighed the jackal. No sooner had he said that, he saw more trouble coming. A tiger! "A tiger is difficult to fool, unlike a leopard. Maybe he can tear the skin for me," thought the clever jackal.

"Hello there! I'm guarding this elephant for the lion but why don't you come and have a piece of it? I will keep a watch and inform you if the lion comes." The tiger liked the idea. He came and tore the skin of the elephant. Just as he was about to bite into it, the jackal yelled, "The lion's here! Hide fast, go, run, he's here!" The poor tiger ran for his life.

The jackal had not only managed to save the carcass for himself but he had also managed to get the skin torn open. He jumped into the flesh, but before he could bite into it, he was stopped by another jackal. Mahachaturaka fought bravely and chased the intruder away. Finally, he was able to eat a feast fit for a king.

Lesson
Different strategies work for different people.

4.8 The Well-Travelled Dog

Chitranga, the dog, finally had enough food to eat to his heart's content. He had travelled a long distance to find food because of the famine situation in his hometown. When humans were dying of starvation, how could a dog survive? He had no option but to travel, and boy, was he glad! He had found a door to a house open, probably because of the carelessness of the house lady. He entered cautiously and to his amazement found a whole lot of delicious goodies. His tail wagged and his ears twitched at the sight of it.

But a full stomach can be a disadvantage too. He learnt that too soon when he stepped out of the house and bumped into the local street dogs

who growled and snarled at him for entering their domain. He tried to escape, but alas, his stomach was too heavy for him to run fast. The dogs caught up to him and left him black and blue.

Happy to be alive, Chitranga realised there was no place like home and headed back to his hometown. His friends and family were relieved to see him and were bursting with questions. "What is it like in a foreign country? Did you get food? How are the people there?"

The well-travelled dog shared what he had learnt. "Women in foreign countries are careless. Yes, there is a lot of food. But the sad part is your own kith and kin behaves like your enemy and tries to kill you," he said sadly.

Lesson

Family and society is intolerant of those who do not follow set rules and cultural norms.

Human tendency is to act first and think later. This leads to a lot of regret and pain because we make judgements before verifying facts. In these stories, we learn to be patient, think and then act. This helps us avoid regrets later in life.

Unlike the last four sections where all characters are birds and animals, characters in the stories from Apariksitakarakam are all humans. This can be seen as an attempt to bring the mind out of the fantasy world, back to the real world, the human world.

Apariksitakarakam

Considered Actions

5.1 The Brave-Hearted Mongoose

"Iwill not let you harm my baby brother, you slithering snake!" said the tiny mongoose to the hissing cobra. He would rather die than allow any harm to come to his baby brother. The cobra was taken aback by the determination of the baby mongoose, although he was much more powerful than him.

The mongoose considered the baby boy in the cradle as his brother. A brother he grew up with. The mongoose had lost his own mother at birth. The boy's father, a Brahmin called Dev Sharma, felt sorry for him and adopted him as his own. His wife had bathed them together and oiled them together. She even fed him her milk as she did to her own son. He always felt grateful to his loving parents for giving him shelter as well as love.

Both mother and father happened to be out and the responsibility of protecting his brother

was on his shoulders alone. Inspired by his loyalty towards his adopted family, he challenged the cobra, his natural enemy.

He bit the cobra in multiple places and finally killed the bleeding reptile. He felt proud of himself and couldn't wait to tell his mother. Just then he heard her footsteps. He rushed out to tell her all that had happened. As soon as the Brahmin's wife saw the bloodstained mongoose, she froze. All her worst fears had materialised. She had never trusted the mongoose because, after all, he was an animal. She had never left her son alone with him. Where was her husband? Assuming that the mongoose had attacked her precious son, she panicked and threw a big stone at him. The mongoose couldn't understand his mother's actions and died instantly.

She rushed inside the house only to see what a terrible mistake she had made. The bloody dead snake showed how bravely the mongoose had fought to save his brother in the cradle. When the Brahmin returned, they could only cry in repentance.

Lesson
Fools act first and think later. The wise think first and act later.

5.2 The Four Treasure-Seekers

"**I** suggest we leave this village, go elsewhere to make money and get rich. What is the use of living like a beggar here?" a poor Brahmin said to his friends. His arguments were persuasive and the other three heartily agreed with him.

After bidding farewell to their circle of friends and relatives, the four Brahmins set off in search of greener pastures. Destiny brought them to a temple on the bank of a river. It was here that they met a wise yogi and they accompanied him to his hermitage. On the way they shared their sorrows with the yogi. "We've been living in abject poverty, on the verge of death. We left in search of money to save ourselves. You are a gifted yogi and must surely have vast powers. Please guide us towards wealth, o' kind yogi."

Another said, "We surrender to you as your followers. We will do whatever you ask of us. Please help us."

The yogi felt compassion for the four poor Brahmins. He indeed had powers that attracted wealth. He wanted to help them. Giving them one wick each he said, "Hold the wick in your hand and walk towards the Himalayas in the north. The path is difficult but holds great treasures."

The yogi explained what they had to do, "When the wick falls from your hand accidentally, know that there is great treasure buried in that exact place. Dig it up and take it home."

The four Brahmins were ecstatic, anticipating that they would soon find great wealth. They hurried to take his blessing and leave. They travelled for many days when one of them dropped the wick accidentally. As instructed, he dug the spot and found a vast amount of treasure of copper statues. He said to his companions, "Friends, we have enough treasure for the four of us. Let us take it and return home." The three friends had a discussion and said, "You may return with your copper treasure. We have greater wealth waiting for us."

The three continued their journey to the Himalayas. Soon enough, another Brahmin dropped his wick accidentally. He dug the spot and, to his joy, found a casket full of silver coins. He said to his friends, "There's enough treasure for the three of us. Let us take it and head home."

The two Brahmins had a discussion and said, "It was your destiny to find silver coins. Perhaps greater wealth is written in our destiny. You are free to return home." The two of them continued the journey, holding wicks in their hands. After a few days, one of them dropped the wick by accident. When he dug the spot, he found a chest full of gold ornaments. Delighted, he turned to his friend, "We were right, we did find greater wealth. It is enough for the two of us. Let us now go home and unite with our friends."

However, the fourth Brahmin was not convinced. He said, "Still greater treasure awaits me. The Himalayas are calling me."

The Brahmin continued alone on his journey. After walking for a few days, he was overcome with fatigue. Hungry and thirsty, he had no clue where he was going. He met a worn out man holding a bulky wheel on his head. He not only looked exhausted but downright sick with blood gushing from his head. He asked the man, "Where can I get water? And who are you? Why are you holding this monstrous wheel over your head?"

Lo and behold, the wheel magically moved from the stranger's head to his head. "Hey hey," the Brahmin cried, "what are you doing? Take your contraption back. I don't want it."

The wheel started spinning on the Brahmin's head as he yelled at the stranger in pain. The stranger, now smiling, said, "This wheel is yours till another man as greedy as you speaks to you holding his wick. Only then will this wheel move from your head to his head.

Many yugas ago I got the wick from the same yogi. Not satisfied with the treasures, I continued to hunt for more and more wealth. And what I got was this wheel. The good thing is that you feel no hunger or thirst; nor ageing or death. But you will feel pain. No one can come here except the one holding the magical wick. Farewell, my friend. I wish you luck." And the man disappeared leaving the Brahmin alone to deal with the consequences of greed.

Lesson
When needs turn into greed, you get only pain and misery.

5.3 The Lion that Sprang to Life

"**O**h please take me with you, I don't want to be left behind!" pleaded the simple Brahmin with his friends. He had no scholarly background and survived only on common sense, but his three friends, who were learned in scriptures, had decided to travel extensively to impress their king, showcase their high end knowledge and earn name and fame. They had planned to leave him behind because he was of no use with his mere common sense!

Being good-hearted, they eventually decided to take him along. He was, after all, their friend. Crossing through a dense jungle, they found a heap of bones, possibly of a lion. What fun it would be to bring alive a lion,

they thought. It would surely impress everyone when the news spread that they had done the impossible. The simple Brahmin was aghast. "Once the lion is alive, won't he eat us all?" he voiced his fear. It was common sense wasn't it? But the three Brahmins ignored him. He was not scholarly like them! "Oh shut up! What do you know?" they said.

The first Brahmin chanted mantras and the bones assembled together. He chanted some more and soon enough the skeleton of the lion was ready. The second Brahmin lit a fire, mumbled some mantras and voila! The skeleton now stood before them covered with flesh and skin. The third Brahmin smirked, closed his eyes, ready to blow life into the lion when the simple Brahmin interrupted him.

"Wait a minute! What are you doing? If he becomes alive he will kill us!" he shouted in disbelief.

"Do you expect us to stop now and allow our knowledge to go waste? You are simply jealous of us," mocked the third Brahmin.

The simple Brahmin quickly used his common
sense and climbed up a tree. He saw the third
Brahmin blow life into the lion from the safety of
the large tree. As soon as the lion came to life, the
three Brahmins cheered at their success and their
unbelievable power of knowledge. In an instant,
the lion pounced on them and killed them. The
simple Brahmin could do nothing to help them.
After the lion left, the fourth Brahmin climbed

179

down and walked back to his village, happy to still be alive.

Lesson

Knowing how to apply knowledge is more important than the knowledge itself.

5.4 Tale of Two Fishes

"**L**ook at the big fishes in this pond. Let us come here for fishing tomorrow," said one fisherman excitedly to his friends as they crossed a small pond. His friends looked at the pond and their eyes widened with amazement. The pond was teeming with fishes, large and small. They all nodded in glee.

Ekabuddhi, a frog, heard the fishermen and saw their nets and huge baskets. He panicked and ran towards his friends, the fishes. He narrated what he had heard, "My friends, the fishermen are coming to our pond tomorrow to catch us. Should we hide? Should we run? Oh god, what should we do?"

The fishes were not too hassled with the news. Sahasrabuddhi, the largest fish in the pond, said, "The fishermen may or may not come. Why panic unnecessarily? Even if they come, I know many tricks

to save myself. I don't care for these fishermen."

Satabuddhi, her friend, concurred with her, "I too can save myself and my family. Why should we leave our home and run? No need to worry, Ekabuddhi!"

But Ekabuddhi was not convinced. He said, "I see danger here. I will leave immediately with my family to another pond."

Just as the frog had heard, the fishermen arrived next morning and cast their nets. Since it was a small pond, they hauled out many fishes, crabs, turtles and frogs, including Sahasrabuddhi  and Satabuddhi! There was no way the big fishes could save themselves and were dead the moment the net was pulled out. In fact, being the biggest fishes, the fishermen carried both of them in their hands as trophies. When Ekabuddhi saw them from a nearby lake, he was saddened to see his friends dead. If only they had heard his warning and acted upon it, they could have saved their lives!

Lesson

Action is the best option in the face of danger.

5.5 The Donkey that Sang

Udhata, the donkey, was bored of eating the same old grass. He yearned for some fresh juicy vegetables to sink his teeth into. One night, when his master left him in the open field to graze, he came upon an idea. Why not break into the neighbouring farms and feast on organic carrots and beetroots? He decided to do just that! It was such a delicious meal that he ventured into neighbouring farms every night for his daily quota of indulgence.

One day he happened to bump into a jackal wandering in the farm. The two got along well and met every night to share their joys and sorrows. The jackal also got the opportunity to feast on the poultry of the farm the donkey had broken into. Together they enjoyed their nightly adventures.

One full moon night, the donkey was overwhelmed by a desire to sing. He asked the jackal, "My dear friend, would you like to hear me sing? My mother always told me I have a melodious voice." The jackal was flabbergasted. Was the donkey out of his mind? It was a sure-shot way of getting caught by the farmers. He said, "Dear donkey, we are thieves, and while stealing we should be as quiet as possible. If the farmers hear your conch-like voice, we will get a good thrashing. So please eat and forget about the singing."

The donkey was annoyed at being rebuked. He said, "It is unfortunate that you do not appreciate music. I am a connoisseur of music and I shall surely sing!"

The jackal ran out of the farm and hid before the donkey began to bray. No sooner had the donkey begun than the farmer woke up and rushed out to see what all the hullabaloo was about. He could see the donkey clearly in the moonlit night and he grabbed a stick to beat him up for trespassing on his farm. The donkey managed to save his life and ran to the safety of his field.

Lesson

Only the foolish fulfil every desire. The wise wait for the right time and place.

5.6 A Pot of Porridge

Swabhavkripna was lying on his cot bursting with joy. His happiness knew no bounds as he fixed his eyes on the round clay pot hanging in front of him. His precious pot was full of porridge! That meant he had enough food to eat, which was very rare indeed. He begged for a living but never did he collect more than a few morsels to fill his stomach. On the days he got a little more, he would still not eat. He would save it for a rainy day.

By the mercy of the lord, he had a whole pot of porridge now which was untouched. Happy and content, he drifted off to sleep. He dreamt that his pot of porridge was so valuable that he sold it for a hundred silver coins. With that money he bought two goats. And soon he had a whole family of goats with multiple kids. He bartered all the goats for some cows and buffaloes. Very soon, his cattle were giving milk. He became a supplier of milk and milk products. His butter and curd became popular in neighbouring villages and demand was always more than supply.

He was finally a wealthy and respectable man in the village. He built himself a palatial house and travelled by a horse-driven chariot. He got many marriage proposals and he chose the daughter of an affluent Brahmin. His marriage was attended by no less than the royal families of the kingdom. Soon he was the father of a beautiful boy he called Soma Sharma. One day, the naughty boy was up to some mischief and he called his wife to handle him. His wife, being busy with chores, was unable to attend to him. This angered the Brahmin so much that he kicked his wife.

In the dream, he kicked his wife, but in the real world he actually kicked his precious pot of porridge. The pot broke instantly and the porridge splattered all over him. He woke up with a start and that was the end of his dream. He had lost all his porridge and there was no wealth either! The poor Brahmin could do nothing but cry.

Lesson

Success comes not by dreaming but by working on your dreams.

5.7 The Two-headed Bird

A long time ago, there was a very strange bird. A bird, the likes of which had never been seen in the past and would never be seen in the future. It was a bird that had two heads!

This unique bird loved to eat. Since it had two mouths, it got to eat double the quantity eaten by normal birds and experience double the taste of a normal bird. It could eat two fruits in two different branches of the same tree simultaneously. While the mouths ate to their relish, the stomach rejoiced to its fullest.

One day, as the bird was seated on the branch of a tall tree, one head of the bird spotted a succulent looking fruit on a branch close to it. Unfortunately that was the only fruit hanging on that tree. While the second head desperately searched for another fruit, the first head of the bird bit into its newfound treasure. After the first bite, the first head exclaimed that it was the best fruit in all of creation. He went on to say that he had never tasted a fruit this tasty before. The second head was highly tempted upon hearing the admiration. He requested just a bite.

Flatly refusing, the first head continued relishing the fruit. He mocked the second head by saying that ultimately it doesn't matter which head eats the fruit as it is going to reach the stomach. Since they shared a common stomach, the second head shouldn't make a big issue of it. The second head was boiling with anger at the sly comment of the first head. It began to hate the arrogant first head. Swallowing the pain of humiliation, the second head decided that it would get revenge at the first chance.

The sought after chance came the very next day. As they were perched on the branch of another tree, the second head came across a fruit that was hanging near it. Looking at that fruit and the first head that was happily glancing around, the second head got an idea. An idea that would be a permanent revenge!

Moving towards the
fruit, the second
head plucked
it and held it
between its beak.
As soon as the first head
saw the fruit in the mouth of the
second head, it began to scream. "No, not
that fruit! It's a highly poisonous one."

The second head loved that reaction. Placing the
fruit on the branch below it, it looked up at the
first head with a sly grin. "I am going to take
revenge on you today by eating this fruit."

The first head panicked. "Don't do that! Since we
share the same stomach, both of us will suffer if
you eat that fruit."

The second head was in no mood to listen to him.
"Shut up! Since I am the one who found this fruit
first, I will be the one to eat this fruit."

As the fruit entered the beak of the second head,
the first head broke into tears. In a matter of
minutes, both the heads began to suffer due to the

poison in their body. The second head voluntarily brought suffering upon itself to teach the first head a lesson in unity.

Lesson
United strength is better than divided strength.

5.8 The Wise Old Monkey

"These old people imagine too many things!" A dynamic young monkey vented to his friends. Living in the royal palace had been pure fun. No worries about food, no worries about predators and no worries about life. Though they were captives in the royal gardens and were pets of the prince, that didn't really bother them. They had their share of fun and frolic even though they

had to tolerate the irritating prince. Most of the captive monkeys were of the same age. Only one of them was a wise old monkey. His advice was becoming too frequent, although it was unsought.

His advice today had irritated them the most. He said, "My young monkeys, I want to give you a warning that may well save your lives. I don't know if you observed the odd behaviour of the two rams that the prince has. One of them particularly is a glutton and gobbles up every food item he lays his eyes on. The cooks in the kitchen are losing their patience. They throw anything they can lay their hands on to shoo away the ram. What if they throw a piece of burning wood? If that happens, then the entire city may catch fire. We should immediately escape from this palace and save our lives."

The young monkeys laughed their hearts out at the imagination of the old monkey. Only a fool would think of giving up the comfortable life they were living. Being mocked by the youngsters, the wise old monkey decided to leave them to their fate. He made an escape when the time was right.

As predicted by the old monkey, the very next day, the cook threw a piece of burning wood at the ram whose wool caught fire instantly. The panicky ram ran all over the place unable to bear the heat of the fire and finally entered the stable. The hay there caught fire and soon all the horses were neighing in the midst of the ragging blaze. After a long struggle, the king's guards managed to put out the fire but only after all the horses had suffered severe burns.

The veterinary doctor recommended that the best treatment to heal the horses' wounds was application of monkey fat. Instantly, all the young monkeys were caught and killed for the treatment.

When the old monkey heard of this ordeal, he felt sad. He was very upset with the king for being so insensitive to the monkeys. Deciding to take revenge on the king for his folly, the old monkey went to the forest where he came across a huge lake. As he began to walk towards the lake, he noticed something strange. There were many animal footprints that led into the lake, but none that came out of it.

Wanting to be cautious, the wise old monkey plucked hollow stems of a lotus plant and used them as a long straw to drink the water from the lake. Suddenly a huge, ferocious looking monster emerged from the middle of the lake. He expressed his joy at the monkey's intelligence. He said that every animal or human who had entered the lake unknowingly had ended up in his belly. But since the old monkey had exhibited great presence of mind, he wanted to offer him a boon.

Immediately the old monkey saw an opportunity to seek his revenge from the king. Making a deal with the monster, the old monkey went back to the kingdom wearing a priceless necklace given to him by the monster. When the king saw the invaluable necklace around the monkey's neck, he inquired about its source. The monkey told the king that he had discovered a mystical lake in which the treasury of Kubera, the treasurer of gods, was hidden. He said that the lake housed unlimited treasures within it. Anyone who entered the lake on an auspicious day of the week could gain all of it. He advised the king to bring all his men and enter the lake to claim the treasure.

Believing the monkey, the king, along with all his men, reached the lake on the prescribed day. The monkey inspired all the men to enter the lake simultaneously from all directions while he asked the king to wait outside. He promised to show the king a special entry point. Soon everyone had entered the lake except the king.

After a long wait, no one seemed to be coming out. The king was confused and asked the monkey for the reason.

The old monkey smiled at the king and said that all of them were now in the belly of the monster. He had avenged the death of all the monkeys the king had killed. The lonely king returned heartbroken.

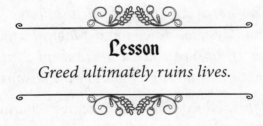

Lesson
Greed ultimately ruins lives.

Author

Shubha Vilas, *author, motivational speaker and storyteller, holds a degree in Engineering and Patent Law, but he chose to leave mainstream society to live a life of contemplation with a deep study of scriptures.*

Apart from Ramayana - The Game of Life series, he has authored Open-Eyed Meditations, Perfect Love, and Mystical Tales for a Magical Life. These books transform Vedic literature and epics into easily relatable stories and contemporary life lessons.

Meaningful education that creates character in children is his key passion. This led him to successfully create a Value Education module which could be incorporated into children's existing syllabi. With this module, he now guides young minds in the right direction, inspiring a life based on values and principles.

The Panchatantra by Shubha Vilas is unlike any other story book because he adds to them his own energy and insights. Every lesson becomes a practical tip that can easily be used by not only children but also adults.